FOR
THE WANT
OF SILVER

MICHAEL E WILLS

First published in 2023 by the author using *Bygone Ages Press*

Copyright © Michael E Wills 2023

ISBN 978-1-739858858 (Paperback)
ISBN 978-1-739297657 (eBook)

British Library Cataloguing in Publication Data
A CIP catalogue record for this book is
available from the British Library

Bygone Ages Press

In memory of my late mother-in-law,
Elsa Dahlgren Palmer. (1921 – 2023).
A champion of equal opportunities for women and
men and an inspirational woman.
I am privileged to have been her friend.

PREFACE

This book is a novel, and as such, it is a work of fiction. However, an historic novel must have respect for the history it is based on. The history of the late tenth and early eleventh centuries in England provides the backbone of this story and, together with evidence described below, the novelist's imagination adds flesh to the bones.

The period in question was extremely turbulent in England and to comprehend it in detail is a scholarly challenge. It was a time of betrayals, battles and brutishness on a large scale. An epoch when those who sought power and wealth clashed violently and almost continuously with those who wished to retain it. The mayhem caused was much to the distress and bewilderment of the citizens of the country. The succession of monarchs in a relatively short period, in order of appearance, illustrates the turbulence: Ethelred, Svein Fork Beard, Knut, Ethelred, (again), Edmund, Knut.

As a novelist it is not my purpose to relate the complexities of the period, but the story requires that from time to time I describe how my main protagonist is involved in some of them.

Much has been written about why the Norse raided other countries so mercilessly. To me, it seems that the main part of the answer has to do with the precarious nature of existence in the cold north and the poverty it inflicted on its inhabitants. The easy pickings offered by poorly defended, relatively wealthy settlements were irresistible to opportunistic adventurers used to a harder life. It can be claimed that the raiders were bestial because they were pagan, but it should be noted that both Svein and his son Knut were Christian. Even the very religious King Ethelred was capable of ordering a pogrom during his reign.

It was during this period that an unwelcome Norseman named Ulf visited England. He was a resident of the hamlet called Borresta, a little north of Stockholm. I use the term *Norseman* in the book, as that is what the men of that period called each other. The word *Viking* did not exist at the time in the sense that it defined a person. This noun came in to use several centuries later. The expression "to go a-viking" was used to describe a piratical activity.

By way of explanation about a feature of the story, Ulf lived in Sweden at a time when two separate ethnic groups, the Geats and the Svea, had almost totally merged. It had taken over four centuries for this process to happen. Yet there were still disputes and feuds between them. The Geats occupied the southern half of the country. Even today there are still traces of their identity. Gothenburg takes its name from a mediaeval form of the word and means "Geat Fortress."

The term "Svea" is still very much in use, for example, weather forecasters use the term "Svealand" to describe the central part of the country.

Ulf was a real person, and further, we know that he occupied himself by "going a-viking." The proof is an inscription on a runestone, meticulously recorded as U344. Today, the stone stands outside the church in the village of Borresta. The runestone briefly relates an extraordinary tale of a man's quest for silver. It is this description that has inspired my novel.

Michael E Wills
Salisbury 2013

INTRODUCTION

My dream was interrupted by a loud curse. The man in front of me had seized a stone chipping to hurl at an animal as it weaved between the tools on the floor and the detritus of his trade. The rat was too quick. First its grey shape, then the long, pink, tapered tail vanished through a gap in the logs of the workshop wall.

It was my turn to curse. I had relied on the tap, tap, tapping to keep me from dozing but after several hours the effect had instead induced sleep. This was my usual time for a nap anyway, but I was determined to keep control of the situation. This was my project, my life, my idea. Had the arthritis not so blighted my joints I would be doing the work, for I was the most skilled rune maker, everyone said so. Or did they say so because I was wealthy, and their livelihoods were in my hands, bent and stiff as my fingers are? The fingers that once could draw a bowstring, grip a sword and caress a woman.

And caress a woman. Yes, I have, though not often enough. And now, and now even when my servant girl leans forward to tuck the blankets round me or creeps into my bed to warm me, I feel nothing. That thrill in my loins that once signalled arousal has deserted me, and the member between my legs lies like a cowardly cur in its uselessness.

"More care man, what are you doing? This rune stone is for me, me, Ulf of Borresta, the greatest traveller after Ingvar the

Far Travelled, not some nameless thrall. Take care if you are to be paid."

Ingvar, yes, Ingvar the Far Travelled. I was fortunate not to have been born ten years earlier for I would certainly have joined his venture to the east. They say that two thousand men, some of them from the lands that became mine, went with him to seek gold in the east. And just six men returned. Six exhausted and sick men, and of gold they had none. My journeys have not been without danger, but my destination was different and the gods or the God has greatly favoured me.

I fought to watch the work and to listen to the tapping to avoid dozing off again. Yes, the gods or the God. Whom to believe? The gods served me well, though not always those who travelled with me. I closed my eyes and pictured Erik, why did the gods not favour him? Or Onäm, for he surely deserved to find favour. But according to the old gods they were favoured, for the belief was that a man should find and rejoice in honour while alive and then perish with courage and the promise of life as a warrior in the afterworld. But then the men with the shaven heads, black robes, and chests decorated with a cross, who do not fight, but instead preach peace and brotherhood, tell us that our reward for following them is an everlasting life of brotherhood, peace, and plenty in a world after death.

Brotherhood, what were we adventurers if not brothers? The dangers of the sea journeys through wind and spume with the crack of the sails and the creak of the timber; the foreboding as we faced an enemy of superior numbers; and the tenderness with which we dressed each other's wounds after the fray. The gathering of the spoils and the sharing of a foaming drinking horn, these were the things that shaped our brotherhood.

And plenty – had I not plenty? My farm is the richest in many a day's march. My henchmen are the strongest and most feared in the region and my family, thralls, and freemen are thus well protected from anyone who would dare to do us ill. And all this is because I, Ulf of Borresta, was brave enough not to be one of the *hemsk* – those who stayed at home and lived a dull existence of toil and poverty. I journeyed over land and sea, fought, bled, and risked everything for the want of silver.

As I laid back, submerging into the furs on my chair, I closed my eyes and felt the raised scar on my neck. It was as always: the vision appeared. The semblance of a woman, a young black-haired woman with dark, alluring eyes, eyes that had captivated me. An image that momentarily blocked all others in my rich memory. And the image did not dim as I aged. As if to taunt me, it increased in clarity with every winter that passed. Deep down, I admitted to myself that I felt remorse, for I knew that my bravado, my bluster, and boastful thoughts were cover, a veil to hide my greatest failure. I was and still am intoxicated by my greed for wealth, but this obsession has caused the subject of my love, the mother of my eldest son and heir, to slip out of reach.

I know that thoughts of her make me morose, I try hard to banish them and to force other recollections to the fore. For unlike the hemsk, I have the richest of memories of any man to immerse myself in.

CHAPTER 1

Borresta, Svealand, the year 983

The ice had formed early that year, too early, but it did mean that we could have fun slipping and sliding, for there had been no snow fall yet, and the ice was completely clear. That is if we dared test its thickness.

Erik was the same age as me, I think, but he was bigger and stronger, though he was not quick witted. In fact, I did not choose him as a friend; he just seemed to follow me everywhere, I think he just wanted to be with someone who was cleverer than him. He was a very good fighter and whenever I got into a brawl with other boys, he always helped me, and we never lost. So, I let him be my friend, but that was only if he helped me with the chores my parents gave me, for he had more spare time than most others. His father, Mundr, was the village smith, and he owned two thralls who helped with the running of his home and the work in the forge.

"Perhaps the ice might hold. But listen. Listen, Erik, they say that the ice forms to cover the shame of the wailing of warriors who have drowned with no honour and won't be accepted by the Valkyries to enter Valhalla, they have been banished to Hel."

"That's stupid, Ulf. Come on, let's try it."

"Careful, we'll walk out slowly."

I let Erik go first; he was heavier than me and if the ice held for him, it would for me. It was not that I was a coward, I was just more careful. I was also immensely curious; the thrill of walking on the very water that a few short weeks earlier I had fished in, was irresistible.

"It's safe, come on, Ulf, come on."

He started to jump up and down to show how solid the ice was.

"Stop, stop, Erik. Look, the ice is so clear that you can see the fish – that is, the ones you haven't frightened away."

Peering through the ice, the weak sun was giving just enough light for us to see perch darting around under us in the shallow water.

"By Odin's beard, what's that!?" shouted Erik, pointing at a dark shape under the ice.

We both gazed down into the water below us. The expressionless, white face pressing up under the ice was that of my grandfather. Aghast, I stared at the figure below me.

"Isn't it your father's old man?"

My voice was trembling as I answered, "Yes, Erik. Father told me he was going on a journey."

"He didn't travel far, did he?"

"Shut up. I'm going home."

Home was a wooden building, a large hut. The timbers had been darkened by the ravages of the weather of many years, and where the original logs had succumbed to the damp, it was patched with rough-hewn planks. The turf on the roof was a dull yellow rendered untidy by some longer grass straws that still challenged the early winter wind. It was in one of two rows of simple dwellings. The lines of houses faced each other. At the end of one row was a long house. There was a time, perhaps when my grandfather's father lived here, when most extended families lived in long houses, but they are expensive to build and cause too many family squabbles, so now most people prefer to have their own house.

The village long house was owned by squint-eyed Sieward, the *bryti*, the foreman appointed by the regional chieftain, who served as the steward to manage the chieftain's estates. Each dwelling had a little land around it. It was used by different owners as they saw fit. Some grew vegetables, some kept fenced-in pigs; others, such as the carpenter, plied their trade there. My father kept a cow that grazed there while there was grass and in the winter lived in a stall that was part of the house. This helped to keep the building warm. The track between the houses was paved with hewn planks resting on logs. At one end of the street, next to the long house, was an open space, used variously as a market, a meeting place, or just for sheep grazing. Beyond this was the forested trail that led out of the village. The other end of the boardwalk led down a slope to the waterside. The villagers were freemen, and most had the right to at least one field. This right, given to their families long ago, was granted by the regional chieftain. There they could grow crops to provide for their own needs. Such land rights were passed down from father to oldest son or, if there were no sons, then to a daughter.

It was a simple though harsh existence. Much of the abundance of each summer was husbanded to provide for the cold months. Nothing went to waste. We were used to living on the edge of starvation, and for generations it had been so. While nature could be cruel beyond imagination, it could also be kind. We had good fishing, and the men folk knew how to trap and hunt. The area we lived in was rich in game, both two- and four-footed.

I scurried off the ice and hurried as best I could to the village. The ground was rutted and uneven where the frost had hardened the muddy footprints of men and cattle, making it very difficult to run. It was easier when I reached the firmer footing of the wooden street. As I hurried, I thought about the last time I had seen my grandfather. It must have been one evening just last week. He had left the house to go to the privy, or at least I believed he had. I thought it was strange that he didn't put on his old wolf skin coat when he had left the room. He took a long time, even though he was always slow; his legs were so weak he could hardly walk. I had become worried. I'd asked Father where he'd got to and he told me that Grandfather had gone on a journey.

My mother was at her loom when I burst in and told her what I had seen. She looked at me calmly and said, "Your father thought that he would spare you this."

"Spare me what?"

"That the time had come for the old man to die."

"But what do you mean? Why?"

"Ulf, your grandfather knew that he was a burden to us. He could neither plough nor fish. He had had his life and he knew that the victuals we save by not having to feed him through the winter could make the difference in keeping the rest of us from starvation."

"So, what did he do then?"

"He walked out on to the thin ice. It would have been a quick end."

At first I was stunned, but on reflection, I remembered talk of old folk and babies, especially deformed ones, being put out, by hungry relatives, into the forest in winter.

"It could have been worse. Some folk throw their old kin off the Skull Cliff."

I knew what mother was referring to. There was a hill outside the village with a precipice on one side. There were dark stories about aged relatives, who had got too burdensome, being pushed over the edge. The wolves cleared up the evidence.

"Ulf, you have to understand. It gives us a better chance to survive the winter. He'd had his life, he wanted to give us ours." She began to sob. "You know how bad things are."

I was well aware that nature had not been good to us that year. It had started badly in the spring, the wild bird egg collecting season, when there were hardly any nests to plunder. In the spring, the snows had melted late and then the rains came and washed away most of what the villagers had planted. The growing season, the summer, seemed to have been very short. Such crops as managed to grow were small and underdeveloped when they had to be harvested before the early frosts. The fruit trees had suffered too. The late frosts had damaged the fruit blossom and there wasn't much to pick in the autumn. As the cold winter approached, most of the families in the village were complaining that their food storage bins were hardly half full.

"Mother, can't we buy more grain from the *bryti*?"

"We have no silver to buy extra food." Then she added, "When you're a man you must go a- viking to lift yourself out of this misery. You should follow the trail of your uncle."

Mother often told me how well my father's brother was doing, but it was only when I was older that I realised that she had not seen or heard from him since he had selfishly abandoned his childhood home to seek a better life. His name was whispered quietly in the village. He was regarded with some disgrace for not staying to help his father in providing for his brother and sisters.

The door opened and Father came in. He looked at me briefly, then at Mother.

She spoke first.

"He knows."

"How do you mean?" he said gruffly.

"I saw Grandfather, his corpse is under the ice."

"He obviously didn't get far out from the shore then," he said more softly, thinking aloud.

My father put his arm round my shoulder and said, "It had to be done, he wouldn't have lived for much longer anyway."

He paused and then said, "One day perhaps your mother and I will have to do the same thing."

"No, Father, for I will have silver, silver to buy grain and perhaps meat."

He gave me a resigned look and said no more before he kicked off his winter boots and threw another log on to the fire.

"At least you can start to fish through the ice now, Ulf, and I hope that you have better fortune than I have had hunting."

He was referring to the long monotonous days he spent in the forest trying to find meat for the table. Every day as darkness fell, he would return tired and hungry, often with nothing to show for his day in the cold.

"I'm not joking, you'll see. One day I'll come home with a bag of silver."

"Stop dreaming, Ulf," he scoffed. "Do something useful, go out to get some more logs from the store."

Our lives were guided by the beliefs that had been handed from father to son and mother to daughter. Sigrid was the *völva* in the village. We children called her Bent Sigrid because she always stooped when she walked, though we were too scared to call her that when she was listening. She had inherited her mother's ability to see into the future on special days. On these occasions, she dressed in bright colours and we children had to sing a chant to help her find the mystic power to foretell things like how good the harvest would be or who would be next to die in the village. She used a handful of thin sticks that she threw into the air. When they hit the ground, she stooped even lower than usual to interpret the meaning of how they had fallen.

At the time of the longest and shortest days of the year Sigrid officiated at the *blot*, the sacrificial feast. She splashed the blood of a sacrificed animal around her house and over the menfolk who had assembled there. This gave the gods strength to combat evil forces, such as the giants who lived in *Utgård*.

My father was very superstitious, and he always carried a charm representing Ullr, the god of archery and hunting. Perhaps it helped him, for two days after we had seen Grandfather's body, he came home dragging the carcass of a roe deer. The animal provided meat for us for several weeks. We ate a little of the meat fresh, but by far the main part went into the large wooden barrel with an iron hearth, at the back of the house, to be smoked. This way it was preserved for the cold weeks ahead.

Nevertheless, our winter diet those years consisted mainly of fish. The scarcity of food on the land was not mirrored by that in the lake. But it was not enough and soon there were stories from travellers about lawless brigands who were raiding isolated homesteads in search of food. We were lucky; there were enough strong men in the village to defend the little we had.

While the monotonous diet of fish did fill our bellies, it did not give us all the goodness we needed and very soon there were illnesses to which the weakest succumbed. We could not bury the dead, for the winter ground was unyielding, so the corpses had to be kept in one of the houses that had belonged to an old couple who had died. This gave the dead protection from the hungry teeth of wolves and other predators that were also suffering from the famine. In the spring it was terrible, for the bodies of the dead corrupted faster than the frozen ground softened to allow graves to be dug.

There were two more harsh years like this one before my life changed forever and for me, hunger became just a bad memory.

The hardships of the villagers were added to by the demands of the local chieftain, Gnir. He required that the tithes should be paid each autumn. We had never seen the chieftain, but his tax collector, Ingemund, came to the village every year. And he did not come alone; he always took two or three armed warriors to protect him and to intimidate those who did not pay willingly.

I remember that year very clearly, for I had reached an age when my shrill childhood voice had been replaced by a lower tone, that of a man.

The sound of the barking village dogs presaged the appearance of Gnir's men through a gap in the pines lining the track into the village. This warning usually gave its occupants a little time in which to hide some of the goods, such as furs and hand tools, that might have attracted Ingemund's greedy attention.

My curiosity frequently got me into trouble and that day was no exception. While many of the children had run into their houses, for fear of the outsiders, I stood with Erik, watching as the procession of horses slowly walked into the clearing at the end of the village. Ingemund rode in front of three armed men. Behind them, another armed man led a horse and cart. In the cart were two large barrels and bundles of furs.

The tax collector sat tall in the saddle as he looked down at the wretched villagers assembled before him. He wore thick, grey woollen trousers bound to his legs below the knee. His leather jerkin had a high collar laced up to his jutting chin. A thick leather belt circled his waist, in front of which was a long knife in a sheath. His face was thin and his high cheek bones seemed to protrude over sunken cheeks partly covered by a sparse grey beard. It was not the face of a generous man.

Squint-eyed Siewert scurried forward to take the bridle of the leader's horse.

"We must talk of the harvest, *bryti*. But first I have business to attend to. Boy, take my horse and find fodder for him," demanded Ingemund of me.

I held the horse by the bridle as Ingemund dismounted. I was not used to looking after horses, for we had none in our village, but I pretended to know what I was doing and led it to the wood store by the side of our house. As I did so, I noticed the fine quality of the decorative bridle and the skilled leather work of the saddle. I was surprised to see that there was a spear lashed to the side of the horse, just under the saddle. I reflected that the group of visitors was very well armed; no doubt they had to guard against being robbed as they traversed the country gathering the taxes. As I tethered the horse, I heard Ingemund shout, "Now men of Borresta, you know the tax, a tub of salt herring and a bear skin or two deer skins from each household."

There was no word of protest. No one dared.

Men turned and went off to their homes, reappearing a while later. Some had thralls with them to help carry the small casks and rolled furs. Others managed alone. Ingemund beckoned to his companions to dismount and help him. Each of them was dressed in a similar fashion to their leader, but unlike him they were armed with swords. They had shields strapped to their backs.

The villagers started placing the wooden casks on the ground in front of the three warriors. When they had all done so, Ingemund said to his men, "Let's have a look at them, then."

He always checked the fish before they were added to those already in the barrels on the cart, the tithes already paid by other villages.

The three armed men started to prise the lids off of the casks, and as they did so Ingemund leaned forward to inspect the contents of each one.

"This is not full, whose is it?"

The villagers looked at each other. They knew what would happen if Ingemund was dissatisfied with the goods; he would consider that he could take anything else he pleased from the household responsible as compensation.

Crooked Nose Arne was pushed forward by the others, none of whom wanted to take the blame for him trying to cheat Ingemund.

"Who are you?" asked Ingemund.

"Arne, son of Arne, sir."

"Where is your house?"

Crooked Nose Arne pointed to one of the grass-roofed cottages. Ingemund looked at one of his men and jerked his head in the direction of the house, indicating that the man should go there.

"No, no, sir, I can fill up the cask," pleaded Arne.

"Too late, Arne," said Ingemund, his scowl breaking into a grin.

All eyes were on the warrior who was striding towards the house. Just in front of the building there was a smouldering pile of wood heaped around an iron container – the patient work of the woman of the house. The man knew that it was a birch bark distiller that collected birch tar to use as ointment. He paused and kicked it over before pushing open the door of Arne's house. Soon there was a scream. The door opened and the warrior strode out carrying an iron cooking pot by the handle. He was pursued by a woman, Arne's wife. She grabbed at the pot to try to retrieve it, but he roughly pushed her away until eventually she gave up and threw her hands up in despair.

"Take the pot," Ingemund instructed. "Now let's look at the furs."

One by one the men of the village untied the rolls of furs. Ingemund inspected each one carefully, but he found no flaws until Father untied the second deer skin. It was one that Erik and I had shot arrows at while it was stretched for drying and scraping. Father had been furious with me, and I remembered vividly the thrashing I had received.

"A pox on you, man, how many arrows did you use to kill the beast, it is riddled with holes!?"

"It didn't die easily, I had to track it after it was wounded."

"Not acceptable. Give me another," demanded Ingemund.

"I have two good hare skins you could take," pleaded Father.

"By the gods, I don't take hare skins. Who are you?"

"Hafnir, son of Bjarne."

"Then take this as an example to those who would cheat me. Which is your house, Hafnir?"

Father hesitated a moment too long in his anxiety not to betray which house was his. One of the warriors swiped the back of his hand across Father's face. I could feel the pain as if it had been my own face.

"There, there, that one," he said as he pointed to the house beside which I was standing, before wiping the blood from his mouth.

Ingemund looked at the warrior who had hit Father and indicated that he should go to our house.

Looking back at my childhood, I cannot remember that I was an unusually violent child. In fact, as I recall, only two things ever brought me to anger: losing wrestling or fighting games, which I frequently did against Erik, and insults to the name of my family. Even then my temper was normally restrained. I suppose that it was on the day of Ingemund's visit that I first experienced real rage. It was as if a mist covered my mind and dimmed the normal instinct of self-preservation. In later life, it was to blot out fear and direct intense hatred at the man who is my enemy.

As the warrior strode towards our house, I dashed around the side of the building to where the horse was grazing. I pulled at the spearhead and the spear slid out from the leather binding that held it. As I carried it into the cow stall at the back house, I remember thinking that it was heavier than I had expected.

My entrance through the back door coincided with the warrior coming through the front into the only other room in the house. He reacted quickly at the sight of me with the spear. He started to draw his sword. As he did so, I jabbed the spear at his face and cut his cheek just below his left eye. Blood immediately flowed down his face and into his brown beard. He howled with either pain or anger, perhaps both. I had to stop him drawing his sword; there was no going back on what I had done. I tried to jab his face again, for I realised that I was not strong enough to push the spear through his jerkin. I was too slow in using the heavy spear. He grabbed the shaft and wrenched it from my hands. He threw it to the floor and, standing balanced with feet apart to maximise the power of his downward stroke, raised his sword over my head. That moment seemed to go on forever. In his eyes I saw a look of hatred, seasoned by the lust for vengeance. I remember that his mouth was half open, showing many gaps in his teeth. There was no escape for me; I was frozen to the spot.

CHAPTER 2

The fury of the warrior and the pain of his wound had clearly confused his brain as he had not considered that the overhead swing of his sword would hit the rafters of the low ceiling. He checked his strike in mid swing as he tangled with the lines of drying herbs and smoked fish hanging from the rafters. He paused to adjust his attack on me to be a sideways swipe.

This gave me the opportunity I needed. My kick at the easy target between the warrior's legs coincided with the front door being thrown open and Erik blocking the light as he blundered through it.

The armed man made a sound that reminded me of the noise pigs make when cornered, something between a squeal and a grunt. He dropped his left hand to protect his privates and with his right started to swing the sword at me. The blow never came; Erik had grabbed one of my mother's loom weights, a heavy hollow circle of dried clay. He smashed it into small pieces over the back of the warrior's head. The man seemed to stand like a pine tree that had received just enough axe cuts to make it tremble as it conceded that it could no longer stand. And just like the tree, he began to topple, at first very slowly and then, as his weight could no longer be carried by weakened legs, he crashed to the floor.

I grabbed the spear and held the point hard into the back of his neck. My heart was thumping and though my brain was consumed with hatred, for the first and only time in my life when I had the power to kill a man, I hesitated.

"Stop! No, no. By the gods, Ulf, stop."

My father had just come through the door, closely followed by Ingemund and two warriors.

"The cursed swine was going to rob our house, Father."

Before he could plead with me again, one of the warriors grabbed him from behind by his hair and pulled his head back. With his other hand he swung his knife hard up against Father's throat.

The sound of the men shouting and my mother screaming confused me, and I found it difficult to think clearly. I wanted to kill the man on the floor, but if I did so the blood would flow from my father's throat. My young mind just could not deal with this.

"Do you want to watch your father have his gizzard slashed, whelp?" growled Ingemund.

Naively I bleated, "Let him go and I will spare the warrior."

Ingemund roared a ghastly laugh and nodded to the man holding Father. The warrior pressed his knife hard enough for a small slit to start oozing blood.

"We must give in Ulf," whispered Erik.

The thought of what retribution would be sought from Erik and me was added to the heady mix of emotions I was already trying to contend with.

The silence in the room probably lasted just for a couple of seconds, but it was a tortuously tense silence as I watched the blood trickle from the underside of Father's beard onto his shirt collar.

I stood up from my position of crouching with the spear held in both hands and threw it to the floor.

There was a loud gasp from my parents, a gasp of relief. This was concurrent with Ingemund shouting, "Seize them, the brats need to be shown what pain is."

It was useless to resist the hefty fellow who wrenched my arm up my back with one hand and stuck his knife hard against my ribs with the other. Erik was foolish enough to aim a kick at the man who grabbed him, and in consequence received a vicious punch to the left cheek, just under his eye.

"Woman, tend to Agmunder. Wash the blood from his head before he wakes, for when he recovers he will be in a murderous temper," demanded Ingemund, pointing to the man on the dirt floor of the room.

As we were pushed out of the house, Mother tried to reach out to me, but Father held her back with a hand covered in blood from his wound. I heard him say, "Leave the damn fool boy, he nearly had us all killed."

"How can you say that, at least he tried to defend what is ours. You just watched as they pilfered the goods of village folk."

Father's retort to this was lost to me as the door swung closed.

The crowd outside the house that had previously only been men, was now swelled by the village womenfolk and children of all ages.

"Make way, stand back!" shouted Ingemund as he led the way across to where the cart stood at the edge of the clearing. "Hold them here while I get rope," he ordered as he marched across to one of the pack animals.

I looked across at Erik, his left cheek swollen and the eye above it almost closed. He grinned at me. It was a stupid reaction to meeting my eye. He showed no fear, but then he didn't realise that we were about to be hung. Or perhaps he did and had not grasped that hanging meant death and that would be the end of everything.

As Ingemund strode back to the cart with a coil of rope, the warrior holding my arm gave it a vicious jerk upwards to remind me that I was to be punished, and that I was defenceless.

Then the warrior released my arm and held me tightly round the throat with his forearm as Ingemund wrapped the rope around my wrists. I was confused; why was he not putting it around my neck? I began to get some hope that I was not to be hung. He lashed me to the cart wheel with my belly hard up against it. The warrior pushed his knife under the collar of my jacket to cut it, and ripped it and my shirt off, leaving my back uncovered.

"Take the other end and tie the big brat to the other wheel," Ingemund ordered the man who was holding Erik.

Soon Erik and I were helplessly bound, facing each other across the back of the cart. A chorus of gasps and comments from the onlookers caught my attention. I turned my head and was terrified to see Ingemund pulling a large hand axe out of a bundle on the back of one of the horses. My imagination was running wild; how was he going to use the axe on us, who would be killed first?

Erik was speaking to me, and I turned back towards him.

"What did you say?"

"I said, it was a good fight, Ulf. Did you see that bastard fall?"

"Oh, shut up, Erik"

I ignored him when he added, "It was a pity we couldn't kill the foul brute."

I looked back towards where Ingemund was standing. He was no longer holding the axe; he had given it to one of the warriors. The man was disappearing towards the track that led out of the village.

My attention was diverted by a scream, and I recognised the tone of my mother's voice. I could not turn my head far enough to see what was happening, but Erik could as he was facing in the other direction.

"What is it, Erik? Why is she screaming?"

"It's the man we fought, he is coming towards us with his sword in his hand. His hair and his face are covered with blood. We did a good job; he must be badly hurt."

"But what is my mother screaming for?"

"She is holding his arm and trying to stop him coming over here."

There was a loud murmur in the crowd and some shouts.

"By the gods, he has hit her with the pommel of his sword. She's fallen to the ground. The man is a lunatic. You should have killed him."

"It was you who told me to stop. But if we survive this, I will kill him."

There was a loud shout, and I recognised the voice of Ingemund.

"Stop, stop, Agmunder. You shall have your chance of revenge but not here."

"I'll have the heads of the filthy thralls!" thundered a voice, obviously that of the wounded warrior.

"The tax collector and the other warrior are holding the bleeding bastard, at least they are trying to," Erik shouted to me above the noise of the crowd.

Just then I saw the man who had gone off with the axe returning, carrying some pine branches. He had obviously seen his master and the warrior wrestling with Agmunder, for he started running to help them.

"What's happening now, Erik?" I asked.

"They are talking to the angry one, trying to calm him."

"Why did the other one bring the pine branches?"

"How should I know? They are cutting some long twigs from the branches for some reason."

Ingemund's voice boomed out again. "Village folk, you have seen what happened today. A housecarl, warrior servant of your chieftain, Agmunder, has been attacked by these two boys. If he had been killed, the death price for a free man, as you all know, would have been more than a hundred aurar[1] of silver. Who would have paid that? You would all have had to forfeit everything you have."

There was a shout from the crowd, "What are you doing with the boys?"

"That was my father, Ulf," whispered Erik.

"The whelps are to be punished by the one they have offended."

"He's waving a pine branch in the air," said Erik.

"Oh no, I understand now, we are to be beaten with the pine branches."

"That can't hurt too much," said Erik.

"Just wait. The pine needles are in small clumps on the twigs, they're sharp."

Agmunder came into my view carrying a length of pine branch. He held it high in the air and whipped it down on to Erik's back. My friend winced as he was struck but made no sound. As Agmunder lifted the branch again, Erik grinned at

---

1 1 Aurar – 28 gms or an ounce

me. Why, oh, why did he grin? That was the last time his lips broke into a smile during his ordeal, but not once, and there were ten strokes, not once did he murmur. Could I be so brave? The challenge for me was to be as courageous as Erik.

It was my turn. I was surprised how heavy the branch was; it pushed me forward into the wheel and almost took my breath away. The sensation was like a very hard slap, and the second was similar but now there was a severe stinging pain as the pine needles found their way into my skin. I leant forward, fighting to stay quiet. I bit the rim of the cart wheel. It was a wooden wheel and my teeth began to sink into the wet timber regardless of the foul taste that exuded from it. The pine branch strokes were punctuated by the heavy gasps of Agmunder, who was clearly breathless from the exertion. In the beginning I counted the strokes but soon my brain was too disorderly. It seemed to go on and on but later Erik told me that I had ten strokes just like him.

"Enough, Agmunder!" It was Ingemund's voice.

The beating stopped and the warriors untied our hands. Erik leaned heavily on the cart wheel in front of him, but I fell backwards and suffered more as my back touched the grass. I looked up, and there, peering down at me, was Agmunder.

"That is your punishment for now. When you are old enough to hold a sword, I will kill you. Our feud will continue until then."

Erik staggered over to where I was laying, held out his hand to help me up, and then, turning to Agmunder, said, "You will have to kill me first."

"As you wish," said Agmunder as he turned and walked over to the village well to wash his bloodied hair.

Both of our fathers rushed over to us as soon as Agmunder had gone. It was then that I saw the state of Erik's back. There were large angry wheals criss-crossing it and several open wounds and smaller cuts. The realisation that my back must look similar made me feel very weak. Soon I felt even weaker and started shaking as the shock effect took hold.

Ingemund appeared next to our fathers and said, "You realise that this business will not stop here, Gnir will want retribution for the dishonour shown to his servant. I must take the boys to apologise to him."

"What, take them from the village?" asked Erik's father.

"Yes, is that what you mean?" enquired my own father.

"It is the only way to avoid punishment for the village," answered Ingemund.

"I don't know, they are so young…"

Ingemund was getting irritated by the fathers' questions.

"It doesn't matter what you think, I'll take them anyway. As angry as I am with them, I can see that they are plucky young fighters. They will be well cared for by Gnir."

"Is there no other way?" asked Father.

"No. Now get the village wise woman to attend to their cuts and bring clothes for them. I'll stay here tonight with my men, and we'll leave with the boys in the morning."

This was the end of my childhood. The next morning, with our backs so sore that we could hardly bear to wear a shirt, Erik and I were roped together and followed Ingemund's horse, on foot. Over the next week, we were led to several distant villages to collect the tithes, sleeping on the ground each night and being treated roughly by the five men. Erik was always cheerful, except when Agmunder was at his most sadistic. Looking back now, I realise that although I had often sneered at my friend because I did not regard him as my equal, in fact I was becoming more and more dependent on him. His resilience, his strength, and complete lack of fear far outweighed his dull wit. With the wisdom that comes with age, I can see that I learned much from him, though he learnt little from me. I miss him, but the story of his passing comes much later.

I also took some wisdom from the event that led to our present sorry state. Primarily, I vowed to consider consequences before I let my rage take over reason and to only risk all when the odds are well in my favour.

At length, the six of us arrived in Aros to hand over the tithes to Gnir. It was a wondrous sight to behold. We walked down the boarded main street alongside the river, past the long row of houses. Each one seemed to be bigger than the last, until we reached a wide-open space. People were rushing to and fro but many tarried to watch the procession led by Ingemund. At length we stopped outside the biggest house I had ever seen. Ingemund got off his horse and handed me the reins. He strode up to the building and banged the hilt of his knife on the door.

CHAPTER 3

Aros, the year 986

We hid behind the pack animals and waited until the door was opened. The woman standing in the doorway was obviously the mistress of the house. On her belt, as well as her knife she had a ribbon with some keys hanging from it. The keys were a clear symbol of her authority in the household. She spoke to Ingemund and then, turning round, called into the house. After a while a man, whose broad shoulders were exaggerated by the sheep skin waistcoat he wore, appeared between the door posts. He had long, grey hair which, together with his beard, framed the features of a powerful face. He had a jutting chin and a large nose. His eyes peered out from under bushy, grey eyebrows.

"Is your work done in the southern province, Ingemund?"

"It is, Jarl Gnir."

"And will the result please me?"

"Undoubtedly, though the freemen of the villages complain that they have little left after paying the tithes."

"It was ever thus. Who are the boys who try to escape my gaze?"

"Two lads from Borresta. They are fine fighters and have asked to serve you."

Gnir sneered and stepped forward to look at us.

"So, young pups, you want to join my band of fighting men?"

I was overawed by the situation and looked at Erik, hesitating about how to reply. He was scuffing the dusty track, peering at his boots.

"Well do you, or don't you?" demanded Gnir.

"Yes, yes, sir, don't we, Erik?"

"Yes, of course, sir."

Gnir looked at Ingemund and scoffed. "You say these lads are good fighters?"

"Yes, undoubtedly."

"How do you know?"

All this time the four warriors had been standing holding their horses, partly obscured by them.

"Agmunder, come here man."

The wounded warrior stepped forward and stood full square in front of Gnir. Ingemund pulled the hair on the left side of Agmunder's head aside, revealing the full extent of the still-bloody wound on his face.

"What in the name of Odin happened to you?"

Agmunder was silent and glowering in anticipation of the humiliation to come.

Ingemund laughed and, pointing at the two boys, said, "It was them."

"A knife wound?" asked Gnir.

"A spear."

"A spear! Where did they get a spear?"

"The smaller one, Ulf, stole it from my horse."

Gnir roared with laughter and then said, "So one of my best warriors was nearly killed by two boys."

He stopped laughing and then said, "This is serious, have they been punished?"

"Yes, sir. Ulf, Erik, take off your shirts and show the chieftain your backs."

We undid our jackets and then, carefully, because of the pain, pulled off the shirts, stained with blood from the still weeping sores.

Gnir stepped down onto the street to get a better look at our wounds.

"Did they scream, Ingemund?"

"Not a sound, sir."

"Mmm, all right, I'll take them. You will get paid the usual sum for slaves."

"But they are not thralls, they are the sons of freemen," protested Ingemund.

"Nevertheless, you will get the amount I said. Take the goods to the tithe barn and come to see me later with a full account of what you have collected."

Beckoning towards Erik and me, he added, "Boys, come with me."

Struggling to put our clothes back on, we followed him into the house. It was a place such as I could never have imagined, with a great hall in the centre and some doors that must have led to other rooms, though we never saw inside them. In the middle of the hall there was an enormous hearth with benches drawn up around it. We nervously swept the room with our eyes. Much of it was too dark for us to make out any detail, having just come in from the bright daylight outside.

"Come here, boys," said Gnir in a friendly fashion.

We stood close up in front of him. He seemed bigger than ever.

Grabbing each of us by an ear, he said, "You young brats are years from being able to join my housecarls. You will work for me, and when I consider that you are ready, you will be trained to fight."

Erik spoke out, as I feared he might. "What work, sir?"

With a raised voice Gnir said, "You will see, but to get the strength to fight you need to do heavy work."

Intimidated by his change of mood, I said, "We can work, sir. We can do any jobs you need done."

Gnir transferred his grip from our ears to pinching both of us hard by holding our chins in his hands. He looked down at us, glowering, and said, "Oh you will, Ulf, you will."

There was a long silence as he stared into our eyes, first Erik's, then mine.

He released his grip, turned towards one of the doors, and called, "Gun, Gun."

A door opened and the woman we had first seen when she opened the door on our arrival, came into the hall, drying her hands on her apron.

"Gun, take these boys to the wise woman and get their backs treated before their blood is poisoned."

As he spoke, he turned us both round so that Gun could see the blood on our shirts.

She nodded and gently pushed us in the direction of the front door, following after us.

As we retreated, Gnir shouted, "Make sure she treats them well, the two of them have cost me six aurar of silver!"

Just as we were about to leave, he called out again. "Oh boys, don't think that Agmunder will forget what you have done. One day he will try to kill you."

Erik and I exchanged glances and then silently went outside and waited for Gun to show us where to go.

This was the one and only time that Gnir showed any kindness to us. He was true to his word about the heavy work we would be expected to do. We were lodged in a barn at the back of Gnir's house. It was next to a long building where his housecarls practised. This building was open on all four sides, the roof being supported by massive upright logs. We shared our lodgings with some of the warriors who were not married. In the daytime, they were busy training and preparing their weapons, and the evenings were often rowdy and sometimes bawdy as the men relaxed after their work. That was the time when we first learned to drink strong ale. For my part I formed no great liking for the brew, though I could hold my ale without shaming myself. Erik, on the other hand, developed a weakness for it. When eventually the men settled for the night, we all slept on the floor by the hearth.

At first, we were both very homesick; even the ever-cheerful Erik longed for his home. However, after a few weeks we accepted our new way of life, for it was not entirely dull. It was thrilling to hear the warriors talking about fights they had been in and the places they had seen. Sometimes, when they were the worse for the drink, they boasted about the spoils they had won and the women they had taken. I am sure that they exaggerated their exploits, but there must have been some truth in their tales because several of them had fine silver bracelets and rings, and all of them had swords, the most expensive weapon a warrior could own. Two of them even had Frankish swords, the strongest and most valuable that silver could buy. They told us that much of the riches they had gained had come from the regular raids Gnir made into the territory of the Geats in the south-west. The more I heard, the more I wanted a share in such spoils.

"Erik, we must do all we can to be accepted to join these men."

"And not go home?"

"No, these men are our family now, brutish as they are."

"What about our parents?"

"We shall become so rich that we will be able to go home to them one day with our bags full of silver. There will be no more hunger for them."

"Yes, we shall get so much silver that we'll need a horse to carry it."

"Or two!"

Meals were prepared in Gnir's kitchen, and each evening Erik and I had to carry the food from the hall to the barn. The chieftain fed his men generously, and we ate well too. Gnir knew that he had to keep his men happy. Chieftains are chosen by the men they lead, and he could not risk that there should be discontent. At first, I did feel guilty, aware that my parents might be starving while I had as much as I could eat, and sometimes I even threw food away. It was such a contrast to the poverty at home, but we had to work for it. Our days started at first cock crow, when we had to draw water from the well in the yard and take filled buckets into the barn for the men to wash. After taking the morning food into the barn we had to clean the floors and bring in stacks of fresh reeds to cover them. Then, unless we were called to do other jobs, in the winter we had to clear snow, and at other times of the year help in the garden. Each evening when the warriors came in, after we had collected the food, we had to clean their boots and wash their clothes.

Often, when we were able to sneak away from our tasks, we watched the fighters practising. It was exciting to see the sword fighting trainer, Onäm, drilling the men. He was a very athletic man, broad but not tall. The speed of his movements was incredible. His dashing swordplay confused his adversaries in training. We occasionally saw Agmunder; his scar was now livid and those who dared called him "scarface." When he saw us, he often made gestures such as drawing his hand across his throat.

At times, when the men were away from the building on exercises in the forest, we tried some of the apparatus they used. Our favourite was the *holmgång*. This was a long, horizontal pole on which the two adversaries sat astride, facing each other. The warriors used heavy sticks to hit each other and try to force their opponent to fall off the pole and into the mud underneath. We filled our jackets with hay, climbed up on the bar, and swung the bulging jackets, each trying to dislodge the other. The way we fought really reflected the difference between us. Erik swung hard using his strength to win. I gripped tightly with my knees to withstand the blow and, while Erik was temporarily out of balance from the effect of the wild swing, I would counter to take advantage of his momentary weakness. Sometimes my tricks worked, sometimes not, but as ever, I did not like losing.

One time, probably the second year we had lived on Gnir's estate, when we were busy on the *holmgång*, we did not hear the approaching footsteps, heavy as they were. Erik swiped at me, and I lost my balance and landed on my back in the mud underneath. As I looked up, I saw a figure I recognised and felt the coldness of a sword under my chin.

"See this scar on my face, whelp? It's the reason that one day you are going to get this through your throat."

Above me I could see what Erik was going to do.

"No, no, Erik. No, don't."

Agmunder looked up and quickly sidestepped as Erik attempted to land on top of him. Now we were both in the mud with a very angry warrior raising his sword above us. As he did so, we heard another voice.

"Agmunder, you piss drinking pig, what in the name of Odin are you doing with the lads?"

"Stay back, Onäm, this is my business."

"Put your sword away, I say."

"Go bugger a sheep, you bastard."

There was the sound of something whooshing through the air and a dull thud as a heavy wooden stick, which the warriors used on the *holmgång*, connected with Agmunder's back, sending him sprawling in the mud beside us.

"You all right, boys?" asked Onäm with his sword now pointing towards Agmunder.

We both nodded and scrambled to our feet.

"You had better keep clear of this man; he is a great fighter but has little self-control. His temper will get him killed one day. Go and get cleaned up. And, boys, tell me if you have more threats from Agmunder."

It was a long time before we dared to go near to the training house again, but then in the third or perhaps the fourth year we were in Gnir's service, things changed for us. I recall that we were clearing snow in the passageway between our lodgings and the big house when he came out wearing a great wolfskin coat. We both stopped to let him pass but he stopped and eyed us up and down.

"I see that the two puppies have become dogs, thanks to the fine food I have to pay for. Time for you both to learn to serve me with the housecarls, we're going raiding in the spring. Tomorrow you start to learn the skills of a warrior. Be in the training house when you have finished serving the morning food."

He turned and walked back into the house. As soon as he was out of sight, Erik slapped me on the back and said, "At last, Ulf, we can learn to fight like the others."

"And campaign in the spring. I wonder where?"

"Perhaps we will go a-viking on the ships!" exclaimed Erik. "And make a fortune in silver!"

With our dreams getting more and more exaggerated, we returned to shovelling the snow.

The next morning, we reported to the training house as instructed. We were surprised that there were some other boys about our age milling around, waiting to be told what to do. We did not have to wait long, for one of the warriors who lived in our lodgings arrived carrying a stack of spears. He put them down on a bench and waved his hand, instructing us to gather round.

"I am Botvig. I have been given the task of making you puppies into warriors."

He picked up one of the spears and, with a loud voice, shouted, "You all have the notion that the Norse fight with swords. Wrong! The most common weapon is the cheapest one – the spear."

There was a buzz of remarks among the boys.

"There are two types of spears, throwing spears like this one." He held up a spear.

He picked up another one and held it up. "And thrusting spears."

He looked round at the young faces watching him and said, "You, the boy with the grey cloak. What's the difference between them?"

Erik struggled to say something and some of the others started to giggle. I felt I must help him and intervened by saying, "The throwing spear is lighter."

"I didn't ask you. What's your name, boy?"

"Ulf, Ulf of Borresta."

"Borresta?"

"Yes."

There was a pause while the instructor reflected on something.

"Yes, the thrusting spear is heavier. It needs to be strong so that it doesn't break when you stick it into an enemy's body or his horse. You see too that the blade is bigger, and one side is very sharp. This will allow you to slash and cut in battle."

Botvig swung the spear round within an arm's length of the listeners to demonstrate the slashing movement. Those at the front recoiled and pushed back at those behind.

"But we are going to start with the throwing spear."

He put the heavy weapon down and picked up the slender one.

"One other difference between the two types of spears is that the metal head on the throwing spear can be pulled off the wooden pole. Anyone know why?"

There was an uneasy silence among the boys. They looked round at each other, hoping to avoid the instructor's eye, lest he should pick on them to answer.

"Come on, use your brains! It's simple. If I throw this spear at a man and it hits him or his shield, one of the enemy can pull it out and throw it back at me. You might get killed by your own spear. So why does the head come off? Come on, come on, how stupid are you all?"

I decided that I would risk answering and hoped that I was right.

"If someone pulls the spear out, they will only get the wooden shaft."

"Right, now we are making some progress."

This was the beginning of a long training to use a simple weapon. We spent hours each day learning to improve distance and accuracy, and the winter was almost over before we were declared ready to join the housecarls.

CHAPTER 4

During our training, Erik and I had got to know the other boys. Some were orphans, others had been thrown out of their families for some misdemeanour. A few were related to the warriors in the housecarls. Most of them were friendly enough, but there were also a few who were constantly aggressive. The fact that I had answered Botvig's questions on the first day led to several of the older boys trying to bully me. Erik dealt with this the only way he knew how – by inflicting a few thick lips and some bloody noses. However, as time went on, I gained respect for the accuracy of my throwing and by the time we had been declared ready for action, I was the undisputed leader of the young spearmen.

We were full of swagger about our skills and kept asking Botvig about when we would see action. It was just before Walpurgis festival, a time when the days were longer and the snow had become a muddy slush, that we young ones were called to join the warriors in the training house. Not only were Gnir's housecarls, the warriors who lived permanently on his estate, there, but also many new faces. We understood that the call had gone out to the villages for each to send two warriors to accompany the housecarls for some special purpose. There was a loud rumble of conversation as the large crowd of perhaps a hundred men waited to be told what that purpose was. The sound of men's voices gradually started to diminish as those near the front saw Gnir marching down the path from the big house. By the time he arrived to face the men, there was absolute silence.

"Men, as you have probably guessed, I have not called you all to be here only for a Walpurgis feast."

There was a hubbub of laughter around the crowd.

"No, I have called you freemen and the housecarls because we have serious business. Last year there were several raids on our territory by the Geats. Farms were looted and burned, freemen were taken as slaves, and women were raped and left to rear Geat brats. These outrages must be avenged."

There was a roar from the men, and with this prompt we spearmen joined in and shouted our support.

Gnir held up his hand to stop the din, and when it was quiet enough for him to be heard, he grabbed his sword from its scabbard and waved it in the air.

"We will row to West Aros and then as soon as the tracks are dry enough, march south-west. We shall seek retribution from the Geats and plunder their villages. You shall all have a share of whatever we take."

The men roared again.

"I will be your leader. Botvig will command the spearsmen and Onäm will lead the swordsmen and the axemen. Agmunder, you are our best archer, you'll lead a group of bowmen, whose task is to guard the pack animals with our supplies. Prepare your weapons and travelling packs. If the weather is good, we will leave in five days' time."

Gnir waited a while for the enthusiasm to die down and then added, "But first, tonight we will celebrate Walpurgis."

I found myself swept along by the general euphoria of the crowd. Looking at the men around me, there was little doubt that they would be a formidable fighting force. But within a short time, I found myself beginning to have anxieties about the venture. Perhaps it was nerves, though it was certainly not cowardice. I realise now that it was a manifestation of the lesson I had learnt from the drubbing I had received at Borresta. *Never risk everything unless the odds are well in your favour.* I was sure that Gnir's men were capable of raiding isolated villages and farms, but I began to wonder if a group the size of ours was big enough to prevail if we came upon an organised force of Geats on their own land. I kept my thoughts to myself and joined the raucous merriment of the Walpurgis feast to celebrate the end of winter and the beginning of spring.

Ten days later, we had left the land of the Svea and were in Geat territory. The campaign began well enough, as I killed my first man. He was an old man who tried to keep us away by firing arrows at us. Three of us threw spears at him, but it was mine that hit him just below the beard. In truth, I believe that he was too lame to run away and was trying to delay us so that his family could escape. I looked at his face as he lay on his back, jerking as he died. His face was contorted, with hate as much as pain. His lips were drawn open and his teeth clenched as he grimaced. I stood looking at him for a while. He could have been someone's grandfather; in fact, it disturbed me that his face had similarities to the one we saw under the ice many years ago.

Erik grabbed me by the shoulder and said, "You got the Geat bastard, well done. Come on, let's see if he had any silver."

I pulled out my spear and cleaned it on the grass while Erik searched the old man's belt pouch.

"Hardly worth killing him, just a piece of old bread and a fire lighter," said Erik as he held up the flint and the striking iron.

I took another look at the man's face, and then we joined the rest of the men. It is said that a man will remember the face of his first sweetheart until the day he dies. I know that to be true. But for me another face I will never forget is that of this old peasant. May I kill a hundred men, and I think I have, he is the one I remember.

We marched for many days traversing forests, hills, and boggy marshland. It was worst in the wetlands. The mosquitoes pestered us day and night. The only relief we got was when we could find yarrow plants. We mashed the leaves and coated our exposed skin with the green paste. This was the only thing that kept the irritating insects away.

We found that the small villages were undefended, and we could easily loot them, but for what? The only things of value we found were ornaments and beads worn by villagers we killed or captured. These were poor people, and only a few of the women had silver bracelets or brooches. By the end of the first month, as we marched south, we took more pigs and cattle than we needed to feed the men, but little else. Gnir, sensing that discontent was growing about the lack of valuable plunder, assured us that we would soon reach a big market town where there were wealthy inhabitants.

For my part, I was beginning to recognise the futility of what we were doing. We were getting the revenge Gnir wanted but gaining nothing much else. It seemed to me too that some of the housecarls' behaviour was foolish, in particular, that after plundering each farmstead or village, we burned it. The great pillars of smoke were an obvious sign, to anyone who could see them, that raiders were approaching. This gave the Geats time to bury or hide their valuables and run into the forest before we arrived. It also gave the local chieftains a warning that we were coming. They might have time to gather their strength to resist us. None of this appeared to shake Gnir's complacency.

However, as we neared the town Gnir had mentioned, we had met no real resistance and we were in good spirits at the end of a sunny day's march. Dusk was falling as our force, brimming with confidence, approached the market town. Several of the men had good singing voices and they could be relied on to break into bawdy song when the prospect of drink, and possibly the chance to find women, was near.

We were following a track that led up a hill. There was a birch forest on either side. I was marching close behind Gnir. The men were labouring up the hill. The singing had stopped, for they needed to save their breath for the physical exertion. I noticed that apart from the tramp of feet, there was an eerie silence. There was no bird song. The evening chorus was missing. Birds had been frightened off. We passed several carts that had been abandoned, the horses having been removed from the traces. It looked as if the owners knew we were coming and had left the slow-moving transports after recovering their valuable animals.

"Come on, lads, the town is on the other side of the hill. We should reach it before dark," called Gnir, turning round to face the men behind him. When he turned back to continue walking, he saw what those of us in the front of the column had just noticed. Three riders had appeared from over the brow of the hill. Their horses were walking slowly in our direction.

"Spearsmen, up to the front!" shouted Gnir.

We hurried up to Gnir's side. My heart was pounding; the riders were now close enough for us to see that they were fully armed warriors. The big man in the middle, to judge by his fine horse and appearance, was obviously the leader. His long hair draped from under his helmet onto his shoulders. They were still too far away for our spears to be thrown with any accuracy, but they were close enough for Gnir's voice to reach.

"Who are you and why do you obstruct our path?" he demanded.

The riders stopped. The man riding the horse in the middle shouted, "I am Toste Skagul, and this is not your path."

There was a buzz of comments around the warriors behind us. I heard someone say, "He may be the famous Toste Skagul, but he is no match for us."

I had never heard of this man, but I knew that "skagul" was a term for someone so skilled in battle that he was favoured by the Valkyries, those who permitted entrance to Valhalla.

Gnir was not impressed and waved his hand to those following him, indicating that they should continue up the hill. As he did so, Toste Skagul called out, "Who are you who dares to offend me?"

"I am Gnir, chieftain of the Aros Svear."

As he spoke, the three riders spurred their horses directly towards us; at the same time a shower of arrows reached us from the forest on both sides of the road. There were screams of pain from those in the column behind me who had been hit and curses of defiance from others.

I was frozen with shock and just stood grasping my spear. I gaped as Toste cantered up to us and, swinging his sword, released a torrent of blood from the side of Gnir's neck, leaving his head hanging at an unnatural angle before he crumpled in a heap on the trackway. I looked left, then right and saw that the bowmen had stepped out of the woods and were pointing loaded bows at us, waiting for Toste's order.

"Lay down your arms or taste another volley of arrows!" shouted Toste.

My eyes were fixed on this warrior commander in front of me. I was too shocked to do anything but watch. Everything was so unreal that I did not see the general scramble behind me as some cast down their weapons and others clambered over the dead, the dying, and the wounded to run back down the track.

"Drop it, drop it, you fool Ulf," said a voice. It was Onäm, who was just behind me. I had forgotten that I was still holding my spear. I threw the weapon to the ground and glanced round. The scene was awful. Onäm was still standing, his sword on the ground in front of him, and Erik was sitting on the track with an arrow protruding from his left arm.

Just then there was a whoosh as the bowmen loosed a flight of arrows at the Svear warriors who had decided to run instead of surrender. The Geats then descended on the survivors while others of their force chased after those trying to escape.

Toste sat on his horse, watching the spectacle in front of him. I stood immediately in front of him waiting for my turn to be slaughtered. Occasionally I turned to cast an anxious glance at the carnage behind me. As far as I could see, there were just four men standing. Apart from me, Onäm, Botvig, and Agmunder were standing with weapons at their feet. The Geat warriors were systematically killing the wounded warriors by cutting their throats or firing an arrow at short range directly into their hearts.

I glanced behind me again and saw that two men were standing over Erik, preparing to dispatch him. He had seen what was happening and struggled to his feet.

"No, no, spare him. Please spare him!" I shouted.

No sooner had I shouted than Erik, with his uninjured arm, swung a punch at one of his intended executioners.

Toste was obviously impressed by his courage and called out to the two men who were to kill Erik, "How bad is his injury?"

"This bad!" shouted one and pulled the arrow out of Erik's arm.

"Ow, you foul smelling toad!" bellowed Erik as the arrowhead barb tore through his flesh.

"Hold, hold. This boy has the fighting spirit we need. Spare him," said Toste, laughing.

"Bring them all here!" shouted one of the other riders.

The five of us were dragged to the side of the track. We waited in silence, apart from Erik who was still cursing the man who had taken the arrow out of his arm. In the gathering gloom we watched while the Geat warriors went round searching the dead Svear men for any belongings of value.

It was just light enough for us to see Toste when he rode up to us and said, "It is a given fact that those who survive longest in battle are the best warriors. So, who are you?"

He paused while his horse fidgeted.

"You, you with the shoulders of a bull, who are you?"

"I am Onäm. Onäm of Borresta. I am the trainer of swordmanship in Gnir's camp."

I was stunned. Why did he mention Borresta? I was distracted and did not hear what Toste asked me.

"Have you no ears, boy? I said, 'Who are you?'"

"I, I'm Ulf of Borresta, son of Hafnir."

"Those from Borresta have been lucky tonight," said Toste to one of his riding companions.

"Fortunate indeed," agreed the other.

"And Ulf of Borresta, why are you here, far from home, in my country?"

"To serve the man who had me trained to be a warrior, sir. But he is dead, killed by a greater chieftain."

"A good answer, boy. And you, you with the bloody arm who almost lost his head tonight?"

"I am Erik of Borresta. I follow Ulf."

The three men on horseback all laughed. "Where is this Borresta? It must be favoured by the gods," said Toste.

"And you?" he said, prodding Agmunder with his sword.

"I am a warrior, I serve whoever pays me."

"And have you been paid well for this campaign?"

"No, sir, this land has no silver that we could find."

"And the last man, what is your name?"

"Botvig, sir. I train the spearsmen."

"So, we have three experienced fighters and two boys."

Toste said something to his companions that we could not hear and then said to us, "You have two choices. Next spring, we are to take an army to Aenglandi with the Norwegian chieftain Ulf Tryggvason. Join my force or stay here as one of the dead Svear."

It was too dark to see the faces of the other four to judge their reactions, but Onäm spoke up.

"We are with you, Toste Skagul."

There were murmurs of agreement from the others.

"Then help my men to drag the bodies off the track and march with us into Skara, the town over the hill. But I should warn you, these Geat warriors will not take kindly to you. Expect a difficult time before they accept you as worthy to join them."

As we were about to start the grisly task, Onäm pulled me to one side and said, "Come, we'll deal with Gnir first."

He had noticed that the Geats had not yet looted Gnir's body. We stood for a moment looking at the contorted corpse. Then Onäm whispered, "Quick, take his sword belt and sword. His weapon is of the finest Frankish type."

The dark hid our action, but I noticed that Onäm also took other things from the body, probably Gnir's silver jewellery. That same darkness prevented us from recognising the dead Svear men who we dragged across the cart ruts in the track and then threw into the edge of the forest. It was just as well we could not see them as some had become firm friends. Onäm ripped the shirt off one of the bodies and used it to wrap around the wound on Erik's arm to stem the blood.

At length, from somewhere in the darkness, Toste shouted, "Come, we shall leave the rest until daylight, if the wolves have left anything of them. Let's move on to Skara."

We joined the procession of Geats walking up the hill and then down the other side towards the town. I made a point of walking next to Onäm.

He said to me, "You shall have my sword and I will take Gnir's."

"Why didn't you tell me that you were from Borresta?"

"Because I wanted you to make your own way in the training. In the same way that I had had to many years ago. Though it was difficult for me, I had to fight for respect."

"I don't understand."

"You might have expected favours from someone who is from your own village."

"I need favours from no one."

"You are too self-assured, Ulf. See what has just happened to us. What did you tell Toste that your father's name is?"

"Hafnir."

"Then it is as I have always thought."

"What does my father have to do with this?"

"You dumbskull, Ulf, have you not understood? I am your uncle."

"You, you mean you are my father's brother?"

"Well, that's what an uncle is."

"Um…but how did you become one of Gnir's men?"

"That is a story of great length."

He dropped his voice and said very softly, "Unless we are accepted by Toste, I will never have time to tell you. Beware, he will be watching us very carefully. And we have to win the trust of the Geat men."

"How can we do that?"

"By showing them that we are as good as they are, Ulf."

"But they have just beaten us."

"We had good Svear fighters with us, but we had a poor leader. He was too confident and careless, and now he is dead. We were just a raiding rabble. These Geats are in a real army with a great leader. If we can follow him, we'll get rich."

"Who is this leader?" I asked.

"Some time ago, almost twenty years I think, he took an army to Aenglandi and slew so many of the Saxons that the king there paid him a great fortune, a Danegeld, to leave in peace. That is why I say that if we follow him, we can get rich."

We both walked on in the dark, and I considered Onäm's words in silence.

CHAPTER 5

Skara, the year 990

I was woken by a kick in the ribs. The only light was that streaming in from the ceiling, through the smoke vent.

"Wake up, you Svea swine. Take the piss bucket out."

In the gloom, a beard and long hair hid most of the features of the man looming above me. I scrambled up, but as I did so the man nudged me so hard that I stumbled over Erik and fell to the ground. There was a roar of laughter from the company of men, who, in various states of sitting or lying on the floor, had observed the occurrence.

Erik grabbed at the man's left leg with his good arm, to try to stop the brute kicking me again. The man responded by landing his foot on my friend's wound.

"Argh! You son of a whore, you will pay for that when I'm recovered!" yelled Erik.

The man clenched both of his fists and leant over Erik.

"You Svea bastard, I'll kill you."

As he raised his right arm, a man behind him grabbed it.

"Easy, easy, Tor. Wait until he is recovered, and then kill him with honour."

Tor's scowl broke into a grin.

"You're right, better do it with honour."

Turning back, he swung a kick at me, which I deftly sidestepped, and he shouted, "Did you hear what I said, take the piss bucket out!"

He pointed to the large wooden bucket with a rope handle the men had used to relieve themselves in during the night.

I did as I was instructed and scurried across to the stinking container.

All the while, Botvig, Onäm, and Agmunder had been sitting by their bed furs, watching. When I came back in with the empty bucket, I went over to them and quietly said, "You did nothing to help me. Why not?"

They looked at each other, and then Onäm whispered, "This is just the beginning, Ulf. The Geats will seek to humiliate us every way they can until they learn to trust and, yes, even respect us."

Botvig added, "Whatever you do, don't lose your temper, lad. And tell that friend of yours, who seems to make threats too easily, that the tongue is an unruly member, and his could lead us all into danger."

In the days that followed, we came to realise that Tor was feared and hated by his comrades. We saw that he could be a vicious bully. No doubt that he was a good fighter, but he was a man for us to avoid.

There was a rattling sound as men unbolted the wooden shutters around walls and pushed them open. A blast of cold air blew through the building, dispelling the foul, stale air of the night. The light revealed the interior of the building to us. Through the open windows we could see that there were several other long houses around a wide yard. We learnt later that the warriors with families lived in these, and the one we were in was for single men.

In our cavernous, long house there were two fires, one in the centre of the building, the purpose of which was to provide some warmth to those inside. It had burnt out during the night. The other, which was blazing, was at the far end of the building next to an array of cooking utensils. There, an old man was busy preparing food.

Very soon, around us there was much movement of men as some hurried to go out to relieve themselves, while others entered with pails of water to wash in. A number stood around, where we had slept on the rush covered ground, folding their bed furs and bundling them up. We could see a growing throng congregating around where the cook was preparing porridge and distributing smoked herring.

When we had packed our bundles, we attempted to make our way through building. We got a foretaste of the animosity we were to endure for weeks. We were pushed, tripped, and generally obstructed as we attempted to follow the example of others. When the five of us eventually reached the cook, it was after being constantly held at the back of the queue for food.

To our surprise, as we stood alone at the serving table with our wooden platters held out, he gave Erik a huge portion of porridge and two extra herrings.

He pointed at Erik's bloody dressing as he whispered, "Better eat that before the others see you. You're going to need extra energy to repair that wound."

My hungry friend ate swiftly as best he could with a weak left arm.

We scraped our platters clean and then joined the other men as they filed outside and milled around in the adjoining yard. They seemed to be waiting for something.

"Everyone out, Birger?" asked a tall man whom we immediately recognised as one of the two horsemen who had been with Toste.

"Yes, even the Svea rats."

"Then let's inspect it. Come, Birger."

We quickly realised that Birger was the senior figure among the warriors lodging in the building, and the other man was his superior.

After a short time, they came out.

"Who emptied the piss pot today?" demanded the taller man.

I hesitated, but I had no choice, I had to answer, "Me, sir."

There were guffaws and comments from the crowd.

"It stinks. Did no one tell you to wash out the bucket after you empty it?"

Before I could answer, he continued, "We'll give you a chance to learn. You will be responsible for the bucket each morning, and you can start by scrubbing the floor around where it stands."

The crowd seemed to like this idea, and there were shouts of approval.

"When you have finished, you can spend the day changing the rushes on the floor. Clean the place out, and then go to the river to cut new ones. The boy with the wound can still swing a reaphook, he'll help you. You other Svea men, come with us, we have graves to dig."

Over the next days the cook was the only person who befriended us. I never learnt his name; everyone called him "Cook" or, sometimes, because of his white hair, "Old Cook." He came to talk to us where we were sitting well out of the way of our tormentors.

"Why do you risk being seen talking with the Svear?" asked Onäm. "You will become unpopular with your comrades."

He laughed and said, "They know better than to become my enemy."

"Why?" I asked.

He giggled and whispered, "Food is what keeps the men happy, and they know that I am the best cook here." He glanced round to see if anyone could hear him, then leant forward and said, "And besides, they know I could poison any of them."

Apart from him, we were isolated and reviled. Onäm was right, our new companions did their utmost to humiliate us and force us into taking reprisals. We were shamed when we were taken to the shore of a lake to have our late comrades' weapons thrown into the water as a sacrifice to Odin to thank him for victory. It was made worse by the laughing and cheering of the Geats. They fought with each other to grab a dead Svear's spear, sword, or bow and then cast it as far as they could into the water. Later we marched to the *Harg*, the cult place. Toste gave the shaman a large silver ring, with smaller ones threaded on it, as an offering. We Svear were pushed forward to hear an admonition from the shaman.

"You butchers of the north who live on the blood of the Geat people. You reviled thieves and rapists, whose misdeeds will be revenged a thousand times over, have been spared by Odin through his servant Toste Skagul. He has given you a chance to redeem yourselves, though you are not worthy to join a Geat army," he croaked.

His speech continued in this vein until Toste signalled by raising his hand that he was satisfied that enough had been said. Then we had to find our way through a booing phalanx of Geat warriors to set off back to the camp.

"At least we were allowed to keep our weapons," Onäm whispered to me as we got clear of the taunting warriors.

"Why did you want to have Gnir's sword?"

"The weapon is a very special one. I don't know how he got it, but I have been envious of it for a long time."

"How is it better than the one you gave me?"

"It is made of the strongest metal called Damascene iron. How it is made is kept a great secret by the makers."

"Who are they?"

"Iron smiths in the Frankish country, far south of our land. They are called Ulfbert."

"Then is the sword you gave me not good?"

"Oh yes, good enough for you. At least it will not bend in combat."

"How do you mean?"

"You'll see, in battle poorer swords are easily bent and rendered useless."

I thought deeply about what he had told me as we walked on to the longhouse.

The humiliation continued. We were tripped, pushed, spat at, and even pissed on to wake us up, but there was never outright violence against us. Even so, some of the games they played were dangerous. One prank even earned a rebuke from Toste. It was when we were about to set off one morning on our way to a battle exercise in the forest. I was dressed in my heavy jacket as it seemed that it might snow during the day. We were each given a small loaf of bread to keep for our midday meal.

"Here, Svea rat, some bread for you to nibble," scoffed a warrior as he passed me the loaf.

I sniffed it to make sure that it was fresh. As I did so, I noticed that many of the men were crowding around to watch me, but I could not see why.

"Put the bread away, lad, we must march," a gruff voice said.

"Come on, hurry up," said another.

I reached for my shoulder bag and started to open it. As I did so I felt a movement inside. I put my hand in and at the same time there was a hiss. I ripped the bag open as wide as possible and out crawled an adder. As I withdrew my hand it struck at me. The wide-open fangs clenched on the sleeve of my jacket.

"Damn you, you bastards. Why are you trying to kill me!?" I shouted. No one heard me, such was the roar of laughter and the jibes. My rage took over. I wanted to kill the perpetrator. I had no weapon to hand, which in view of the number of men around me was perhaps just as well, so I used the snake.

I grabbed the creature by the tail and slung it at the crowd. The mass of taunting men parted to avoid the venomous bite, but as they did so Toste appeared from behind them. He looked at me and then at the coiled adder and shouted, "You fools, to try the patience of the Svear men is natural, but if anyone kills one, they will pay dear. We need all the good men we have for our journey next year. Enough of these dangerous games."

We formed up outside and set off, and I walked alongside Onäm. Erik and Botvig were behind us and Agmunder in front. I was still seething with anger.

"You were lucky, Ulf. The weather is cold, and the snake was dozy, ready for its winter sleep."

"It could have killed me."

"No, not a strong lad like you, but if it had bitten you, you wouldn't have been marching for a few days."

I lowered my voice and said, "What will these Geat swine do next? I could have killed the bastard who put that in my bag."

"It was a good thing that you didn't try, for I fancy that we might all have been dead by now. Swine or not, they are our new comrades now. I don't think they will harm us after the threat from Toste," answered Onäm.

"Are you sure?" I asked.

"Yes, they will just play their games, foul as they are, until they tire of them," said Onäm.

"And how long before they weary of making us look stupid?" asked Erik.

"The more they learn to trust us as fighters, the sooner they will treat us as equals," said Botvig.

Agmunder, who seldom contributed to our conversation, added, "We could challenge them to a contest."

"And give them a chance to kill us all?" I said.

Onäm said enthusiastically, "No, Agmunder is right, Ulf. We could issue a challenge. Man on man in our best skills. We could offer a contest with you and Botvig against their two best spearsman, Agmunder against their best bowman, me against their leading swordsman."

"What about me?" pleaded Erik.

"Um...what can you do with one good arm?" asked Botvig.

"He could challenge their best arm wrestler," I suggested.

"My arm is almost healed now, I could join with Agmunder. I'm good with a bow, ask Ulf."

"No, arm wrestling for you, Erik," said Onäm.

We all laughed and continued to plan how we could arrange such a contest.

When we had thought the whole thing through and decided on the challenges, Onäm sought out Toste Skagul. We followed him to the leader's hut. There was a guard standing by the door, and when he saw us approaching, he drew his sword.

"What do you Svear rats want?" demanded the guard.

"I want to speak with Toste Skagul," Onäm replied calmly, but loudly enough for his voice to penetrate the door of the hut.

"He has no business with the likes of you," said the guard as he waved us away from the hut.

The door opened and Toste bent down to pass through the low opening.

"What are you all doing here?" he asked.

"I have a matter I wish to discuss with you, Toste Skagul," answered Onäm.

The leader stood silently for a few seconds; he was clearly intrigued by Onäm's request. Turning to look at the guard, he said, "Take his sword and knife and let him pass."

Onäm handed over the weapons and then followed Toste into the hut, leaving the door open. The rest of us waited outside, but we could hear the conversation easily enough.

"We tire of the way your men treat us," ventured Onäm.

There was the sound of chuckling.

"Would you prefer to be left in a ditch like the others in your murderous mob?" growled Toste.

"No, I can see why your army is successful. We want to be part of it."

"Do you think that you are all good enough?"

"Yes, I do, and we want to prove it."

"How?"

"A challenge, the five of us would contest with your best men in different skills."

"Which skills?"

"Archery, spearsmanship, arm wrestling, and the sword."

Toste roared with laughter and slapped his hand against his thigh.

"Aye, you shall have your contest, the men need some distraction. But I want no killing, I need every man we've got, even you five. This shall be a contest of skills, not strength."

When Onäm came out of the hut, we crowded round him to ask about how the challenge was to be arranged.

"Come over to the trees away from the tents where we can't be overheard."

When we got there, we gathered around my uncle to listen to his plan.

"I have agreed with Toste how we should do this."

"How? When?" I asked.

Onäm proceeded to explain how the challenge would be organised. When he had finished, he looked around at us and said, "There is one important thing that you must remember."

"What's that?" asked Botvig.

"You must not win."

The four of us looked aghast and then beset Onäm with questions. He held up his hand and said, "You must not win, for if you do so there will be more hate for us than we already suffer. You must be as good as you can be to impress the Geats, but do not win. You hear me?"

There were groans and some protests, then Onäm's voice became threatening.

"Do you hear me?"

Resentfully, we nodded in agreement.

On the day set for the contest the weather was very cold, and frost covered the grass in the morning. Winter was fast approaching. As soon as the frost had cleared, preparations were made for the four contests. A thin rope was stretched down the trunk of a tree, flat against it. Another was tied around the tree to cross the first. This was to be the target for the spearsmen and the archers. A bench was made for the arm wrestling and a square marked out for the swordsmen.

The spear throwing was the first contest. After some discussion it was agreed that the spearsmen would throw, from forty paces, to try to hit the rope.

Toste himself stood in front of the crowd and explained the rules.

"Each man will throw two spears, one after the other. The spear coming nearest to where the two ropes cross is the winner."

As there was a roar of approval from the spectators, Onäm leant forward and said to Botvig and me, "Remember what I told you."

We both nodded.

Toste came forward with the two Geat warriors who were going to throw.

"I will cut a notch in the spears of the Svear men so that there is no doubt which are theirs. You, you the boy, what's your name?"

"Ulf, sir."

"I am putting my knife behind my back."

He pulled the knife out of the sheath and held it behind him.

"Am I holding it by the handle or the blade?"

I thought for a moment and then realised what was happening, Toste was letting this decide who should throw first, a Geat or a Svear.

"The blade, sir."

He brought his arm round and we saw that he was holding the handle of the knife.

"One of my men starts and then one of yours follows."

The first of the Geat throwers pitched his spears. The first one missed the tree altogether, much to the amusement of the onlookers, but the second pierced the tree to the side of the vertical rope by about the span of a hand, and about the same distance below the other horizontal one. A huge cheer went up from the crowd.

Botvig leant towards me and said, "You go next, Ulf, but unless you want a thrashing, don't better that one."

I was very nervous. I had to do well for the honour of the Svea, but not too well.

As my spear disappeared into the forest, having missed the tree completely, the spectators started to chant insults at me. My nervousness began to change into a rage as I prepared to throw. I would stop the insults by showing them what I could do. I glanced at Onäm; he knew what was going through my mind. He scowled at me and shook his head.

My spear hit the tree just below that of the Geats. The chanting stopped and turned to cheering as the second Geat warrior stepped up to throw. I caught Onäm's eye; this time he smiled as he shook his head.

Both of the next two spears thudded into the tree, but they were lower than the winning one.

Now was Botvig's turn to impress without winning. The crowd was silent. His first spear glanced off of the last one to be thrown and fell to the ground to the accompaniment of shouts of derision. He looked at me and said, "Now we show them."

I was terrified. Had he decided to ignore Onäm's order?

The spear did not thud into the tree, for it was so accurately cast that it hit the downward rope just below the winning spear and cut through it. A huge cheer went up. Although the cheer was for the winner, it was possible that some applauded Botvig's skill.

Botvig offered his hand to the winning warrior who, after some hesitation, took it and grinned at him. I held my hand out and was likewise treated.

The arm wrestling was next, but it really was no match, for the Geats pitched their strongest five men, one after another, to take on Erik. Though he was a big lad, he was almost dwarfed by several of the five and stood no chance. The result was that he got more and more angry, and the strength of his curses increased with each match.

The archery used the same target as the spears after the rope had been repaired. Agmunder showed similar skill to Botvig in impressing without winning.

"It was a fair match, Agmunder, but the best man has won," called Toste as the last arrow was fired, and they all peered at the arrows peppered on the tree. The Geats' arrows had a red colour on the feathered flights so that they could easily be identified. Neither man had got nearer than a hand's breadth from the cross of the ropes, but the Geats' arrows were easily the closest.

As Toste spoke, they heard a thud as another arrow hit the tree.

"Who in the name of Thor was that?" bellowed Toste.

Erik realised that he had made a big mistake and tried to hide the bow behind him. He was seized by two men and dragged before Toste.

"Was it not shame enough for you to lose your bouts without interfering with another's contest!? shouted the leader.

There was a mixture of curses and guffaws from the crowd.

"But he shoots well," called the winner of the contest.

Toste turned to look at the tree.

"By the gods he does too," he agreed.

Erik's arrow was just inside the angle where the ropes crossed.

Toste looked across at Onäm and joked, "You let the wrong man represent you!"

There was laughter in the crowd, which Toste hushed before saying, "Nevertheless, the contest was won by our man!"

Now the crowd eagerly moved across to the area that had been marked out for the swordsmen. This was the contest they had all been looking forward to most of all. As we pushed through the throng, Botvig pointed to the sky and said to me, "It looks as if they will be fighting in the rain."

It was true; the dark clouds looked very threatening.

"I hope that this is not a bad omen," I answered.

CHAPTER 6

Toste waited until the two swordsmen were by his side and then bellowed at the crowd, "I have commanded that no one should be killed; I need all my men for our spring campaign. The fighters will use oak swords. There is only one rule – they must stay inside the marked square. The man who capitulates is the loser."

The Svear all gathered around Onäm as he stepped away from Toste. He passed his tunic to me, saying, "I won't need this for a while."

He picked up his shield and sword and strode to the centre of the square. There, waiting for him, was the Geat warrior they called "Wolverine," or "Wolve" for short. Men said that he had that name because, like the animal, he could kill prey bigger than himself, and he had shown this in battle. He stood with his distinctive blue and white striped shield held loosely by his side with the heavy oaken sword in the other hand, looking menacingly at Onäm. He wore a short chain-mail shirt and had a curtain of chain mail on the back of his helmet to protect his neck.

"Wolve looks much taller than Onäm," commented Erik.

"Yes, his longer arms will give him an advantage in keeping Onäm at a distance," replied Botvig.

"But Onäm is broader and perhaps stronger," added Erik.

Agmunder said nothing. I looked round at him and began to wonder if, remembering the beating Onäm had once given him when he attacked Erik and me, he wanted Onäm to be hurt and humiliated.

"It will be difficult for Onäm to let Wolve win. He will lose honour," I said.

"We have no honour in the eyes of the Geats," interjected Agmunder unexpectedly.

"I am not so sure, they have seen today what we can do," argued Botvig.

The two men stood shield to shield in the centre of the square, the bosses in the centre of shields making a metallic thud as they met. Each man stared deep into the eyes of the other, waiting for Toste to allow them to start. The sky was getting darker, and snowflakes were beginning to fall.

"Let the match commence!" shouted Toste. A roar went up from the crowd as they jostled to get a view of the fight.

Onäm pushed Wolve away to get room to swing his sword. Both men prodded at each other's shields. Then, first Wolve and then Onäm swung their swords at each other. They both parried with their shields. After doing this several times, Onäm took the other man by surprise when he quickly reversed the direction of the swing. There was a thud as his sword made a glancing blow on Wolve's helmet. The taller man hesitated a second to recover and Onäm moved with unexpected speed to Wolve's right, the side most difficult to protect with a shield. A blow to Wolve's shoulder silenced the crowd.

"He is doing too well!" said Botvig.

"He seems to have forgotten his order to us," I replied.

Onäm's speed of movement was confusing Wolve and clearly making him angry. He snarled curses at his opponent and lashed out wildly. Onäm was methodical and used his incredible agility to stay clear of the wild swings of the sword. This was necessary as the force of them would have caused terrible injury even though the sword was made of oak.

As they fought, the snowstorm developed in intensity and soon those spectators at the back of the crowd could neither be seen nor see the spectacle. By now the square in which the men were fighting was becoming very slushy. The slipperiness of the surface began to limit the way in which Onäm could exploit his speed of movement.

"Agh!" exclaimed the crowd as Wolve failed to connect with a swinging blow. The inertia of the sword caused him to get off balance and slip on the slush. As he fell, he dropped his sword in an effort to break his fall by putting his arm towards the ground.

The Geat lay on his back in the slush, now unarmed. There were shouts from the back of the crowd asking what had happened and curses from those at the front as they told him to get up and defend himself.

Onäm leapt forward but instead of holding his own sword against his opponent's throat to demand surrender, he kicked his opponent's sword towards Wolve so that he could reach it. He put his own sword under his arm and stretched out his hand to offer it to help Wolve to his feet.

There was a storm of cheers from the crowd as they realised that the bout would continue. However, their optimism was short lived.

Toste stepped into the square and pushed himself between the two men.

"Enough, enough. There is no point in continuing in this weather. Someone may break a leg or worse."

There were some boos from the crowd, but a glare from Toste at the noisy ones soon silenced these.

"The match is a draw. Both men could have continued, but it would have been foolish to do so," he called out.

Botvig looked at me and said, "A good solution."

"But Onäm was clearly winning and could have been the victor if he had chosen," I complained.

"Yes, but this way we keep peace with the Geats and Onäm's honour is increased. That is good for all of us."

As he spoke, Toste shouted, "Now we shall all celebrate our successes today with an ale!"

"Let's see what the bastards have got to say about the fight," growled Agamund.

"Don't dare to be so stupid as to goad them, Agamund," said Onäm as he joined us. Despite the cold, he was wet with sweat.

"Give me the tunic, Ulf, before my sweat freezes. Now let's see if any of the Geats will join us for a horn of strong ale."

And many of them did, all swapping views about the day's action. There was no doubt that we had won some respect among most of the Geats, though there were still a few who it seemed would always harbour their hatred and mistrust, foremost among them Tor, who continued to torment all of us and in particular Erik.

With the winter increasingly limiting training activities, our attention was turned to the necessity of surviving the hungry time of the year. Although many supplies could be obtained by buying goods stored in the town, Toste was careful not to draw on this source too much and risk coming into conflict with the people who lived there by reducing their stocks. In particular, he was careful not to offend the community of shaven head priests, who had built what they called a holy place. The men told us that more and more people in the town had abandoned the Asa gods and were following the religion the black robed men preached.

To avoid using local supplies, Toste regularly sent us off in hunting parties to look for game in the massive forests surrounding the town. In the days when we were not hunting, we felled trees, as there was a constant need to supplement the stock of firewood that the men had laid up in the autumn.

Nevertheless, we had more time to sit around in the long house, playing dice and other games. Despite the fact that gambling was forbidden, as it often led to violence among the men, disputes sometimes broke out, some ending in brawls. We Svear kept well clear of them as we knew that there was a good chance that we might be singled out for trouble. Strong ale was forbidden too, but many of the men used houses in the town where strong drink and female company were available.

Several of the warriors were great story tellers and often we sat in groups listening to sagas and stories of past exploits. Ofttimes, the older men related tales of past campaigns with Toste Skagul. We listened avidly to these descriptions of past deeds. The old cook was especially good at holding everyone's rapt attention. So good was he that he was often asked to repeat those we had already heard, in particular that of when Toste had joined the great Norwegian warrior Olaf Tryggvason in raids across the Norse Sea. We heard the extraordinary story about how the Norwegian had escaped death many times in the land of the Rus and Wendland as a boy and how as a man, he had plundered Gotland, the Hebrides, the Scilly Isles, and many other places. Now, he was wealthy and powerful but still hungry for more riches and next spring Toste's men were to join him.

"The only time he was afraid was when a shaven head sage on the Scilly Isles predicted that he would soon be seriously wounded when some of his crew conspired against him, but that he would survive and recover," related the old cook.

"And obviously, he did," said Onäm,

"Yes, but he had been near death."

"Why wasn't he killed?" asked Erik.

"Those of his crew who were loyal overcame the mutineers before they could deal a death blow."

"The seer had powerful witchcraft," I said.

"Too powerful. Olaf was so impressed by his foretelling that he asked for baptism in the new religion," interrupted Tor who punctuated his speech by spitting towards the ground. Whether it was intentional or not I don't know, but it provoked an angry reaction from Erik.

"You stupid bastard, keep your spittle off my feet!" exclaimed Erik.

"I'll spit where I want and if you get in the way, that is your problem."

As he spoke, Tor drew his knife from the sheath on his belt.

"I told you before that I was going to kill you."

He held the point of the knife under Erik's chin.

"That time will be coming soon."

All of us carried knives, but only Onäm got his out quickly. He held it against Tor's neck and hissed, "Leave the lad, he meant no harm."

Both men slowly retracted their arms and put their knives away. Tor spat again, this time deliberately on Erik's leg, then turned and walked away.

Later, when he saw me sitting on a log with Onäm and Erik, out of earshot of the other men, Cook sauntered back to join us.

"Erik, you have too ready a temper. If you are not careful it will get you killed."

"Better be killed like a wild bull than a tame rabbit."

"Don't be stupid, or that fluff on your chin will never have the chance to become a beard," retorted Onäm.

"So, what shall we do?" I asked. "Just accept his insults?"

Cook leant forward and said quietly, "Yes, for the moment. But you have to plan to kill Tor before he kills Erik."

"Do you think he will?"

"Yes, Ulf, he will. But he won't do it while we are here or probably not on the march to the coast either. It would incur the wrath of Toste."

"So, when?" asked Erik.

"Either on the ship, where many are drowned by accidentally slipping on the deck and falling over the side, or, most likely, he will wait until we are in action."

"In battle?" I asked.

"Yes, as you will one day see, in battles the situation is often very confused and it is easy to kill your comrades by mistake. Only it wouldn't be a mistake."

There was a long silence while Erik and I considered what had been said.

I broke the silence. "And you are sure he is serious about killing Erik?"

"I know this man; he is vicious and without honour or conscience. He will probably try to kill you too."

"So, I have Agamund and Tor after my blood!"

"Oh, you are under threat from your own kind too, are you?" asked Cook.

Onäm laughed and said, "That was the danger of me training him to use a sword. Agamund swore that when Ulf was properly armed, he would challenge him."

"You think he will soon? He often taunts me with his sword," I said.

"I hope not, for you still have much to learn and muscles to develop."

"If he kills me, your nephew, you will have a blood feud with him."

"Perhaps that is what is keeping him from challenging you."

Onäm stood up and walked away.

"Erik, we have to do something. We must kill them before they kill us."

"Just give me your sword and I will chop Tor's head off."

"Don't be stupid. Listen, the best way to get a man killed is to have someone else do it for you. Otherwise, if you must do it yourself, it is said that there are three chances to kill a man with little danger to the killer," said Cook.

He had our keen attention.

"What are these three ways?" asked Erik.

"They are when a man is at his weakest. When he is sleeping, when he is squatting to empty his bowels, or when he lies between a woman's legs and pleasures himself. At such times a knife can easily be drawn across his throat from behind. But as I say, the best way is to get someone to do the killing for you."

"But how could this be done?" I asked.

"I can tell you, but if you ever mention this to anyone it will be your throats that get cut," whispered the old man.

Cook glanced around to see that he was not overheard and then leant forward and began to tell us what might be done.

CHAPTER 7

The threats from Agamund continued through the winter. From time to time, as he sharpened and polished his sword after exercises, he took a delight in pointing it at Erik and me. Sometimes, when he knew we were looking at him he would wipe his hand over the livid scar, from the spear thrust I had inflicted on him, and look at us threateningly. I knew that he would not use physical violence against us so long as Onäm was around, but I was conscious of what Cook had said about the dangers of him fixing an "accident" for us on the ship. Or beyond that, when we were in action in Aenglandi.

Tor's manner with us, and with Erik in particular, was always abusive and he frequently irritated us in many ways, such as him pushing us out of the way as we were queueing for food; barging into our shoulders as he passed us; or putting a foot out.

"He wants you to lose your temper and react so that he can have an excuse to attack you," Cook told us on several occasions. It was all I could do to stop Erik hitting out, but I calmed him by reminding him that we were going to get even with the Geat in a way that was safe for us.

Things had got easier in the long house when winter started. A number of the men left to spend the cold season in their villages. Quite a few of them were married with families. With fewer occupants, and consequently, more space, there was less chance of conflict. However, there were some serious fights.

These were not with us but between some of the warriors who had personal feuds.

Toste recognised that if his men were to fight together, the personal scores between them had to be settled. He allowed men to do this after stripping them of their weapons. Most of the conflicts related to honour, often where one warrior had seriously insulted another. These cases were settled in wrestling bouts or fist fights. The latter could be brutal. Each combatant had his supporters and when these fights took place they were within a circle of loudly shouting men. We kept well clear because, occasionally, fights broke out between the supporters and things got out of hand until Toste sent some of his guards to stop the riot.

There was a serious feud concerning a man who had seduced another man's sister and left her alone with child. Toste allowed the men to fight with the oaken training swords, but the fighters caused such injury to each other that the guards stopped the fight, and it was declared that honour had been restored.

The winter seemed to go on forever and life became increasingly boring.

"Not long now, Ulf. The days are longer, and the snow is turning to slush," declared Onäm.

"It's already difficult to walk on the melting ice to cut reeds at the river. My feet get wet each time I go. By the gods it will be good to leave this foul place," I replied.

"The lice will miss you!" said the old cook who had come to join us.

"And the rats will too," commented Erik.

"How long before we go?" I asked.

"It could be at the time of mid-summer. We have to wait until all the ships are ready to sail," replied the cook.

I was exasperated. "Not until then. Why does it take so long?"

The cook laughed and said, "You know nothing of ships, young Ulf. It takes a great while to prepare a ship for sea after it's been laid up through the winter. There will be an army of carpenters, ropemakers, iron workers, shipwrights, tar distillers, and sailmakers working from dawn to dusk. You have no idea how long it takes to make a sail, or how much wool is needed. If this raid is like the last one there will be more than eighty ships to be made ready. Some of them will then have to sail from different places to meet up at the great western fortress."

The cook's speech did nothing to improve our humour.

"The leaves could be falling from the trees before we reach Aenglandi," quipped Onäm.

"That could be. Then we might have to stay there through the winter," said Cook.

"Is that possible?" I asked.

"Oh yes, many times Norsemen have overwintered there. The good thing is that it is not as cold as it is here."

The cook's words had given us much to think about and to discuss in the weeks to come.

As spring transformed into summer, messengers brought Toste news of the fleet's preparation, and he assembled the men on several occasions to relay the information about delays to us. The messages were received with increasing impatience by the men.

It was in fact well past mid-summer before we finally left the longhouses. On the third day of our march from Skara to the Geat fortress on the coast where we would meet up with Olaf Tryggvason's fleet and board ship, I decided we had to take our chance to silence one of our tormentors. That evening the weather was fine, and we were spending the night outdoors. We had camped by a stream on the edge of a wood. The men were in high spirits; excitement was building about joining the fleet. Toste, who was no less affected, had called up the supply carts that were lumbering along at the end of our column and asked for one of the ale carts to be brought up to where the cook's fire was burning. The drink started to flow and soon there was much laughter and merriment.

Erik and I were sitting on some rocks eating our porridge and salt herring, watching the men around the fire.

"Difficult for you to watch other men drinking, Erik? You'll get none tonight," I joked, knowing his weakness for the ale.

"All the more reason to get this over with so that I don't miss the next feast," he said grumpily.

"You keep your eye on Agamund, and note where he lays his blanket to sleep," I said.

"When he does. This feasting could go on until the cock crows."

"No, Erik, the way they are drinking it won't be long before the ale butts are empty."

"What are you going to do?" asked Erik.

"I saw that Tor has put his sleeping fur and his weapons next to the ash tree by the bend in the stream. I'll watch to see when he goes to bed."

The wait seemed very long, but eventually the crowd around the fire began to disperse and the sound of voices died down. After a while the only sound was the snores of men and the rush of the stream bearing the snow melt towards the sea.

"Come on, then," I said.

"To Tor?"

"Yes, to Tor. Creep slowly and try not to step on the twigs under the trees."

We carefully made our way around the outside of the encampment until in the firelight we could see that we were near to where Tor was sleeping. There was no doubt that with the effect of the ale, he was very soundly asleep.

"Wait here," I whispered to Erik.

I continued to walk as quietly as I could to the recumbent figure. I could see that his spear and sword were protruding from underneath his shield, which was on the ground by his bed. Although I could not see it in in the poor light, I knew that it was his sword from the feel of the distinctive pommel with a cross of Odin mounted on it. The thought occurred to me that Cook was right about when men are helpless, for while Tor slept it was a good opportunity to slash his throat. I reminded myself that we had a different plan and gently lifted his shield so that I could slide the sword out. I crept back to where Erik was waiting, Tor's sword in my hand. We then retraced our steps. When we reached the trees, I took the handle of the sword and Erik carefully held the end of the blade. We put the flat edge against a tree and both of us pushed against it. The sword began to bend and after a while it was almost bent double.

"Agamund is over here," whispered Erik.

He grabbed my arm and led me between the rows of sleeping figures to where the man who was threatening my life was as vulnerable as a kitten and snoring loudly. I had the thought that I could easily kill him too, but the sword in my hand reminded me that we had to see this thing through.

I lifted Agamund's shield and slowly placed the bent sword alongside his own, making sure that the distinctivly shaped pommel was protruding and would be easily seen in the morning light. Then the two of us took our fur rolls and laid them out by our bags. Sleep did not come easily as we were both very excited to see what the morning would bring.

It was at first light that we heard the howl of oaths. There was no mistaking Tor's voice.

"What in the name of the evil one have you done to my sword, you Svea bastard?"

"What d'you mean," growled Agamund as he started to raise himself from his sleeping furs.

Erik and I sat up and watched as Tor swung his fist and hit Agamund, who was still crouching, on the cheek. The Svea warrior was obviously stung by the blow. He rubbed his cheek with his left hand, and as he did so, his right hand fumbled at his belt. He jumped up, his knife in hand. Tor stepped back and reached for his own knife.

By this time a crowd was gathering around the two men, and we had to stand up and get closer to see what was happening.

"No one accuses me of theft and lives!" shouted Agamund as he lunged at Tor.

"You are a damned thief and 'ere the sun rises I shall dance on your corpse," answered the Geat.

They circled round each other, knives held at waist height and, with their left hands raised, ready to grapple with the knife arm of their adversary. Several times each of them attempted to slash the other and each time the other jerked back just out of range.

"Agh!" exclaimed Tor as Agamund's blade caught his left ear and traversed his face. Blood immediately bubbled through the clean cut and started to run down his cheek and into the mass of hair on his face.

Agamund made the mistake of stepping back to see the effect of his strike. As he did so, Tor leapt at him, and the full weight of Tor's charge was added to the inertia of his backward movement. As they fell, Agamund was almost out of sight under Tor, but we saw the Geat's elbow moving back and forth as he plunged his knife into Agamund's body several times. Then they were still and the crowd that had gathered fell silent as they waited for the victor to honour the vanquished and put him out of his dying pain by cutting his throat.

"Did you not hear my order! You hotheaded fool! I said there was to be no killing."

A tall, grey-haired figure had forced his way through the throng of onlookers. As Tor began to raise himself up from the ground, blood now trickling from his beard, Toste kicked him hard in the chest, pushing him back to the ground in a sitting position. The chieftain levelled his sword at Tor's throat.

"By the gods, I've a notion to bury you with Agamund."

The level of excitement in the crowd was intense as Erik turned to me and said, "Good work, we'll get them both killed before breakfast."

"Shut up, you stupid bastard," I hissed at him.

Fortunately, it did not seem that anyone had heard him. I nervously looked behind me just to check, and there was Cook. He looked at me seriously and shook his head. Clearly, he had heard.

"The Svea bastard stole my sword," bleated Tor with an uncharacteristic lack of bluster.

He pointed to the bent weapon on the ground.

"We can replace swords, but not good men. You are a fool, Tor, the fewer men we have the more danger there is for all of us."

He put his sword back in the scabbard and bent down to pick up the ruined weapon.

"A curious thing to do indeed, but then some men cannot hold their drink and their brains become addled."

Tor stood up and glanced round to look at the bloody form of the man on the ground.

"You shall pay for his grave to be dug. Get them to do it," instructed Toste, pointing at some locals who had come to sell their produce to the warriors. "We have no time, we leave after the men have eaten. When we have plunder, you'll pay me twenty auror of silver, the death money for one of my men."

Toste turned and strode off, still seething with anger.

Tor wiped his bloody face with his sleeve and glowered at Erik and me. I realised that we were showing too much interest, grabbed Erik's arm, and took him away from the scene of the fight.

"Let's get some food. Toste has said that we will reach the Geats' fort on the coast in two days; we still have a long march ahead of us."

CHAPTER 8

Gothenburg, the year 991

As we stood on the quay waiting for our turn to embark, it seemed to me that Erik and I were the only ones who had never been to sea before.

"You look scared, lad," said one of the men beside me loudly. He clapped me on the back and turned to his fellows, shouting, "We've got two here who have never tasted the salt before!"

There was laughter and a string of comments.

"See if they can keep their breakfast down."

"The sea'll harden the babes."

"If they don't die of fright first."

The two of us smiled and tried to show such bravado as we could muster, but both of us had seen how the wind was whipping the sea in front of us into white crests, what we later learnt the sailors called "white horses."

We watched as Toste went on board Olaf Tryggvason's great ship and the Geat warriors were shared around the vessels that needed crew. Eventually, one of the rowing boats ferrying warriors out to the anchored ships stopped below the quay in front of us. A voice called up, "Jump, lads, one at a time."

Erik leapt first and managed to stay upright on the heaving boat. I mistimed my jump and landed as the vessel was dropping in the swell. I fell over a thwart, and to the amusement of the onlookers, ended up sitting in the scuppers where there was a pool of water from the spray that had come over the bow earlier. Wet and angry, I climbed over the thwarts where the rowers were sitting and joined Erik, who was in the stern.

By the time there were ten of us on board, one of the shore crew passed our bags and weapons down to the ferry crew for them to be stowed. We cast off and the boat was turned by the oarsmen to head for a ship with one blue and one orange stripe painted around the hull. We could see that the figure head was a dragon.

"What is our ship called?" asked one of the warriors.

"*Dragon*, you can see the bow, can't you?" a crew member answered sarcastically.

The warrior ignored the comment and said, "And the captain?"

There was laughter among the rowers.

"Leif."

"Though most call him Old Thunder."

"Why?"

"You'll soon see," said one rower.

"Hear, you mean," said another amid a chorus of laughter.

As the small boat came alongside the *Dragon*, crew on the ship took a bow and stern line and held them tight as we scrambled on board.

"Hurry, get a move on, land crabs, we have to catch the tide," boomed a voice from the stern of the vessel.

Once we were on board the owner of the voice came forward and shouted, "Let's have a look at you. You, the big chap, take the oar over there." He pointed to one of the rowing thwarts that was not occupied and Onäm made his way towards it. The captain continued placing our companions until there was only Erik and me left.

"You two young lads, take the thwarts nearest the stern where I can keep an eye on you. I'll make sailors of you."

We stumbled over the goods and weapons on the deck, as yet unstowed, and made our way to the thwarts nearest the stern. I took the one on the starboard side and Erik the other. Bearing in mind the warnings we had had about "accidents" at sea, I was relieved to see that we were to be some distance from Tor, who had been placed by the mast.

"Come on. Come on. Get a move on. Hang your shields on the outside of the hull." He pointed to an iron hook on the outside of the gunnel. Both of us scrambled to obey the order.

"Make sure you wedge them tightly or the first wave to hit the side will carry them away."

"What about our bags and rain cloaks?" I asked.

There was laughter from the others sitting nearby.

"Look around you, lad, the crew put their things under their thwarts. That bench you sit on is your home while we are at sea. You eat on it, row on it and sleep on it."

By this time, we knew why Captain Leif was called "Old Thunder". He bellowed even louder when he called to the men in the rowing boat. "That's it. We have a full complement of men. We weigh anchor when the ebb starts."

There was the sound of the captain's orders being relayed to the dinghy and a muffled call from a man in the small boat as they shoved off and started rowing for the shore.

The captain stood up on the small afterdeck and surveyed the crew in front of him. It had already become clear to me that there would be no more taunting of us by the Geats, for now we were in the company of men from many foreign places. There were Slavs, Fresians, Rus, and even two men who were completely black. Since I was on the thwart closest to the stern, I got a good view of the man who would guide us to Aenglandi. He was not a tall man, but he had a chest like an ale barrel. He stood with his hands on his hips, his elbows lifting his rough brown cloak so that it was open at the front, showing that he was wearing a leather jerkin underneath. In the middle of his chest was a large silver hammer of Thor hanging on a leather thong. His grey linen trousers covered the top of his boots. On his head, he had a wide-brimmed black hat protruding from which was his long, grey hair. A string hung down from each side of his hat and later I saw why, for had he not tied the two pieces together under his chin, the hat would soon have blown away. His face was gnarled and weather beaten with many lines and wrinkles. The latter seemed to multiply when he grinned or grimaced.

"Well, crew, we have some new shipmates. They have much to learn, so before we leave, let's tell them the essential things they need to know so that they don't wreck us before we lose sight of land."

There were some guffaws and comments from behind me and then my sea learning began. The captain was right: there was much to know.

Not long after, there was the sound of a horn being blown. The lead ship, which we had been told was carrying Olav Tryggvason, rowed past us. Captain Leif shouted orders, none of which meant anything to me, and men scurried to the bow to haul up the anchor. Soon, I had my first experience of how heavy an oar was.

Fortunately, we did not need to row for long, for with a south-easterly wind, under sail the fleet made good progress on their course. By the second morning in the open sea, Leif told us that we had covered almost half of our voyage. The wind became even more favourable as it shifted to the east and then to the north-east. But then I became aware of some mutterings of concern from the crew members sitting behind me. I noticed that the captain looked at the sky frequently and scanned the horizon.

The man sitting on the thwart behind me, who I later realized was a habitual complainer, leant forward and growled in my ear, "The weather's up to no good when the wind changes against the way the sun goes." I turned to look at him, and he pointed up at the sky to the high cloud formation where there were many wisps with curled tails.

"What does it mean?" I asked.

"Wouldn't surprise me if it goes on round to blow on our faces soon," said the man.

And the wind did continue to go round the compass, but the sun was shining, and we were making good progress. But then, later in the day, the wind dropped. The sea, which was rolling the boat with a gentle swell, had a smooth, almost oily surface. The sun was slowly being extinguished by high cloud and was surrounded by several halos of light.

I sensed apprehension as we waited to see what orders the captain would give. Were we to start rowing or would he wait to see if the wind returned and, if so, from which direction?

"Make fast all the barrels and your gear on deck," bellowed the man in front of me.

I turned to see what the experienced members of the crew were doing and could see that they were lashing moveable equipment and food barrels to the hull beams. Some of the men opened the chests under their seats to get out their heavy rain cloaks. Erik and I did the same. *Dragon* was in sight of several vessels, and I could see other crews busy making similar preparations.

A breeze started to pick up from the north, bringing with it ominous, heavy grey cloud. But the wind direction was favourable, and we continued to sail on our course. Erik and I copied the other rowers we could see and rested at our oars, which we had pulled part way in. All seemed well for some time, and we began to relax again.

"Put in one reef," commanded Leif.

We turned to watch as the sail trimmers lowered the horizontal spar that supported the billowing red and white sail. What they were doing was obscured from us as they were behind the sail, but I understood that they were rolling up the bottom and tying the thin ropes that hung from the sail so that it diminished in size. When they had finished, they hoisted the spar again. Looking around us, I could see that other ships were doing the same, and it was beginning to be obvious why. I could feel on my face the breeze increasing in strength. Very shortly, the benign swell began to deteriorate into waves hitting us on the beam and rolling the *Dragon* more and more dramatically.

"Next reef!" roared the captain against the growl of the wind.

Crew had anticipated his command and were already in place. The breeze became stiffer and the waves, which had been lapping against the side of the ship, were now finding their way further up the hull, and occasionally water would slop over the gunnels and reach the crew on the starboard side.

I turned and anxiously asked the man behind me, "How far is it to land?"

"A long way I hope," he replied.

"Why? Why do you say that?" asked Erik.

The speaker grinned, showing a row of teeth interspersed with gaps. "We're safer out in deep water in a storm than being near a coast."

Leif had overheard what was said. "You scared, lads?" he commented in a voice that made no effort to conceal his sarcasm from those nearest.

There were guffaws and rude comments from others behind us.

"Farmers should stay in the mud where they belong."

"Your mothers can't help you here."

"They've got wet britches and it ain't sea water."

The confidence of the crew in their ship and the captain reassured us, but I could not confess to the others, for fear of being shamed, that I was feeling sick and increasingly so. At that point none of us newcomers realised that this was just the prelude to the main act of the storm.

The increasingly thick cloud cover hastened the dusk, and nightfall found the ship running on a southerly course with shortened sail. I realise now that the captain had difficult choices to make. His dilemma was that if the wind continued to back round to the south, the storm would hit us on the bow. We had three options. We could turn back and run with the wind, losing the voyage progress that we had made in the last day, or perhaps two days, depending on how long the storm lasted. Or, we could continue to sail forward with a deeply reefed sail as close as we dared to the wind, either to the south-west or south-east. To the south-east were the Frisian Islands where we might well be driven on to a lee shore. To the west was the rocky coast of Scotland. Leif must have felt certain that the rest of the captains would not choose the first alternative unless their ships were damaged. So, which of the second and third alternatives should he choose, east or west? He made his decision in the hope that the storm would blow itself out before daylight when he would be able to look for other ships and possibly see land.

The wind did change. It was threatening to blow dead against us.

"Turn west!" shouted Leif with a voice which, though it was meant for the steersman, was also intended for as many crew as possible to hear, to give them reassurance.

As the southerly wind got stronger and stronger, it started to rain. Soon a blend of rain and spray flew over the bow and drenched even those of us sitting in the stern. The wind screamed in the shrouds and rattled anything it found that was not tightly secured. The progress of the ship was halted by the waves rolling and pitching it relentlessly. The oaths from the steersman in front of us betrayed that he was having extreme difficulty controlling the *Dragon*.

"Put in the last reef!" Leif bellowed to sail trimmers in front of him, whom he could not see, but he knew would be there. Then he added, "Man the oars!"

Unseen by us, the sail-trimmers fought with the wild sail, which was flapping madly as the wind was trying to tear it from the spar.

"Starboard rowers, pull!" shouted the now familiar voice. A drum beat from the stern indicated the rhythm for us as we tried to turn the vessel into the wind so that the sail would not fill and trimmers could get it rolled up.

Several other crew members attempted to assist in handing in the sail and taming it. Of the sailors who tried to help, we later heard that two were never to sit at their oars again, their cries for help, as the sea carried them away from the ship, inaudible in the demonic cacophony of the wind and ocean.

There was a shout that echoed down towards the stern by those who heard it, "Reefed, Captain!"

"Ship oars and stow them," was the next order as the *Dragon* turned back to her westerly course.

With the wind now blasting on the port side of the ship she leaned alarmingly, and I became terrifyingly aware that in sitting on the starboard side, the sea was extremely close. I was almost level with it. The hull was being forced into foaming waves as the ship surged along, bucking and twisting at the mercy of the weather. I couldn't see Erik or anyone else and I hoped that they couldn't see me as I retched and threw up at my feet while holding on to the thwart as tightly as I could to prevent being thrown into the sea.

"Starboard rowers move over to the port side, send the message down!" the captain called.

It was immediately obvious that he wanted to put more weight on the windward side to try to stop the vessel being blown over. I clawed my way across and sat on the deck wedged between Erik's legs. Despite this, the breaking waves sent sheets of saltwater over the gunnels and continued to drench the sailors, while the unrelenting wind whipped a maelstrom of rain across the deck. It was as well that members of the crew could not see each other in the dark for there must have been many faces betraying abject terror, which were hidden by the cloak of night.

Then came the order I was dreading, "Bailers, go forward and aft!"

"Come on, Erik, hold on to my coat. Let's go," I said as I squeezed myself out of my relatively secure position.

"Oh no, I feel so damned sick."

"Shut up. Follow me."

I felt him grab the tail of my coat as I half crawled towards the stern.

Early on in the voyage, Leif had chosen us as bailers. "You are small enough to get into the hole, Ulf," he had said. He was referring to compartments called well-rooms where sailors detailed for the work had to creep in to fill buckets with sea water that had drained into the bilges. The person in the well passed the buckets up for them to be emptied over the side. It seemed an easy enough task, but that was in fair weather.

"That you, Erik?" demanded the captain.

"No, he is behind me."

"Put this loop of rope round him in case he gets washed overboard."

I could see the point: the man who emptied the buckets over the side would have a very precarious job.

"Down you go, lad, and hurry. We have shipped a lot of water."

I felt for the lid of the well-room, opened it, and clambered in. I was immediately up to my waist in water, which was surging back and forth as the ship rolled. The water was so deep that it almost pushed me off my feet as it swirled around.

"Here's the bucket, get to it, boy," demanded Leif.

I dipped the bucket into the water, filled it, and quickly realised that when it was completely full I could only just lift it up to the waiting hands of Erik.

"Ulf, next one!" shouted Erik as he pushed the empty bucket back down to me. I repeated the process and then again, and then again until, when I was almost totally exhausted and my legs and feet so cold that I could not feel them, the captain shouted down to me, "Come up, Ulf! Arvid will take over."

Leif had realised that I was working more and more slowly as tiredness overtook me.

"Is the water lower?"

"About the same as when I started, Captain."

"Good, then we are keeping up with it."

When I tried to get out of the well, I was pleased to feel a strong pair of hands drag me up onto the deck. I lay there for a while, sliding around as the ship moved, before I was ordered to go back to the place where I had previously been sitting. Despite the cold in my bones, I felt huge relief to be back in a relatively comfortable place.

By dawn, we were all suffering from nervous and physical exhaustion as well as hunger. But now at least, we could see through the rain squalls that we were not nearing a dangerous coastline. The wind was dropping, and we gradually changed our course further towards south-west. The waves were still high, and as we rode over the top of the crests we could see, far to our east, that we were not the only ones to have survived the storm. Rolling along on the heavy swell were six or seven other ships on a similar course.

"Stay on this course, they'll follow," ordered the captain.

"Where are all the other ships?" Erik shouted to Leif.

"They'll find us, when we sight the coast, we'll stop where the land reaches far out to sea."

It was as he had said. When we sighted land, we continued down the coast until we saw that it bulged out in front of us. There we lowered the sail and just drifted with the pull of the water, which changed in direction several times in the day. The other ships joined us, and gradually more and more appeared until by the time the dim sun was at its height, the sea was crowded and we had to take care not to drift into each other.

"There's Tryggvason's sail!" shouted one of the crew.

We all turned and saw the billowing sail of a large ship heading towards us from the north. There was an image on it, which as the ship got closer we saw was that of a bolt of lightning. Following behind were many other ships.

"He's not stopping. Hoist the sail and follow!" bellowed Leif.

The crew leaped into action. Experienced oarsmen turned us round to face the wind, so that the sail could be hoisted. Erik and I were far too slow to help, but when we realised what was happening, we joined in the effort to bring the ship round on course. Soon we were in the huge fleet of ships, all heading to hug the coast as we sailed south.

"What's happening now?" asked Erik, who, like me, had noticed that the lead ship had struck its sail and was being rowed in to the coast.

The oarsman behind him said, "Tryggvason's looking for a safe anchorage for us to spend the night. It's too late in the day for us to attack whatever place is on the shore."

Just before dusk the huge fleet was gathered at anchor in a river. When we had come in from the sea we saw that there were two rivers; one went to the north-west and the other to the south-west. Tryggvason chose the latter. Many of the ships anchored side by side, so crowded was the anchorage. It could have been a night for a great reunion of old friends and doubtless some enemies, for we could have walked from boat to boat, but a strict order had been given that we were to be quiet and to do nothing to betray our presence. In the half dark, I saw that a rowing boat came alongside the stern, and, in low tones, Leif received his orders from the commander. Whatever he had heard, he kept to himself. All of us knew, however, that tomorrow we would see action. Had it not been for the lack of sleep from the previous night, I would have slept nervously, knowing that the next day I might kill or be killed.

CHAPTER 9

Ipswich, the year 991

"Get your oar, do you want to get rich or not?" asked a gruff but quiet voice.

It was just light enough for me to see that Captain Leif was standing over me as I sat on the deck with my back resting on my thwart. The position in which I had slept all night.

"What are we going to do?" I asked stupidly as I struggled to my feet. Erik was already sitting on his thwart, and in the weak dawn light I could see others were doing the same.

"We are going a-viking, Ulf, you lazy beggar. Cook is coming round with the porridge."

I stood on the gunnel to relieve myself over the side and then grabbed my wooden bowl as the cook stood by with the ladle.

I just had time to scrape the last of the gruel from the bowl when Leif, by stretching his arm and lifting it vertically, indicated to the forward crew to raise the anchor. He ordered us to turn the ship and we followed the fleet seawards before turning into the river, which led north-east.

There were so many ships ahead of us that we could hardly see the town by the waterside.

"Blast it, there's not enough room for us in the harbour," said Leif uncharacteristically quietly to the steersman. "Head for the reed bed over there, we'll have to wade ashore."

As the ship grounded after pushing its way through the dense reeds, we shipped oars and grabbed our weapons. Those who had chain mail were struggling to get the heavy jackets over their heads. Erik and I did not wait for them.

"By the gods, this mud is difficult to walk on," complained Erik as we battled our way through the reeds to a track beyond.

"This way!" shouted Botvig as he passed, spear in hand. We ran as best we could with our boots full of mud. The smoke of hearth fires could be seen rising from the houses beyond clumps of bushes, and we could hear the whoops and howls of the Norse crews as they climbed over the wooden stockade we had also encountered. Several of us managed to pull out some of the poles and make a gap to get through.

Inside, the chaos was unbelievable. Women, some with babes in arms and others with children grasping at their skirts, ran out of their huts and tried to escape landwards. At the same time, their menfolk, most with no shields and little clothing on, wielded axes, scythes, reaphooks and anything else with a sharp edge, in a hopeless attempt to stem the tide of the Norse. A flock of sheep had been released from a pen to hinder the path of the attackers, and these mingled with loosed pigs. The squeals of the pigs, the screams of the women, the bleat of the sheep, the clang of metal against metal, the screeches of defenders as they were hacked down, the wail of terrorised children and the curses and bellowing war cries of the attackers combined to make a dreadful cacophony. As Erik and I stood watching the scene, I occasionally half-heartedly slashed at villagers who passed us, trying to escape, but they deftly evaded my sword. A shout nearby made me turn around.

"We've arrived too late," said Onäm, who had just caught up with us, together with Tor, Wolve and some others.

"There are too damned many of us for such a small place," answered Botvig. "Let's look on the other side of the town to see if there is anything left to take."

We walked past the huts, ignoring the snivelling children and the screams of women and spread out among the farm buildings on the edge of the town. We were followed by marauding warriors as they sought to find anything of value or perhaps a woman to take.

"Erik, let's get away from this madness. Shall we go up to the mill?" I said, pointing to a windmill on a low hill a long distance away from the other buildings.

"Yes, the miller will be rich," he answered.

"At least there might be some food there."

"Yes, I am famished. I didn't get my fair share of gruel this morning."

We waved to Botvig to show where we were going; he saw our departure but obviously preferred to stay in the village. Unseen by us, someone else had noted where we were going. We broke into a run, the mud still squelching in our boots. Erik was carrying his bow and I, my sword. Glancing behind I saw that no one else had seemed to show an interest in the place of our attention.

As we neared the building, we saw a man climbing onto a horse. He held the end of a rope, on which a donkey was tethered. The large woman sitting on the small animal seemed a curious match. Long before we could reach them, the man kicked his heels into his animal's sides, and it immediately broke into a trot.

As the rope tightened the donkey gave a loud honk of protest before it followed, attempting to keep the horse's pace.

"Can you reach them with an arrow, Erik?" I asked.

"Perhaps."

We stopped, and he put an arrow in his bow, quickly stretched the twine, and let the arrow fly. We watched as it traversed the distance and fell just short of the donkey.

"I'll try again," said Erik.

"How many arrows have you got?"

"Nine left."

"Best keep them in case the miller comes back with help."

"What do we do now?"

"Let's look at the mill, there must be things worth plundering," I replied.

Thinking back on it now, I realise how stupid we were. Just the two of us with no support, further inside Saxon territory than our compatriots. Lacking experience and exhilarated by the hunt, but without a care, we approached the building that stood beside the windmill.

Seeing that there was a hole for a key in the door, and without trying first to see if the door was unlocked, I said, "Kick in the door, Erik."

One kick and the door flew open to the accompaniment of a woman's screams. Overtaken with bravado, we were both determined to be first to ransack the property. I led the way through the opening, sword in hand. At first, we saw nothing, our eyes not yet accustomed to the half dark inside, but we could hear a woman sobbing with terror.

Erik saw her first, a grey-haired woman, cowering in a corner by a couch, pleading for mercy with her hands held up. Her plaits hung down, each on one side of the simple dress she was wearing. She looked to be a servant in the house. Judging from the quantity of food on the table, she had just served a morning meal for the miller and his wife. An old man leaning on a crutch hobbled between Erik and the woman. He was unarmed and harmless, but clearly wanted to protect her. I looked at Erik, wondering if he would kill the brave man and actually hoped that he would not. Instead, he turned to me and put his sword away. He started laughing. The absurdity of the situation was obvious, and his violent aggression dissipated quickly, especially at the sight of the food. He grabbed a stool, sat down, and grabbed a chunk of bread. I did the same as the woman picked up a knife and started to cut slices of meat from a large joint at the end of the table.

"I'm thirsty," said Erik.

"There's milk there," I said, pointing to a jug.

"No, I need a beer."

He turned to the old man and said, "Ale?"

As he did so, he mimed lifting a glass to his lips.

The man grinned and beckoned Erik to follow him. I watched through the unshuttered window as the old man hobbled across the yard, followed by Erik. They went into a small building with a chimney. I realised that this was probably the brew house.

The old woman sat awkwardly on a bench watching me as I continued eating. I did not know that I was also being watched by someone else, through the cracks in a door. After a while I became uneasy, for I had noticed that the old woman was nervously casting glances at a door near the end of the room that had previously escaped my attention. I got up and walked over to it. She put her hand to her mouth in horror.

I tried to push the door open, but it did not give. There was no lock on the outside, so there had to be something inside preventing me from entering. I took a step back and then threw all my weight forward against it. There was the sound of wood cracking; a catch must have given way. I pushed the door aside and entered. Despite the poor light, I could see that there, crouching on the floor close to the door, with one arm crossed over her head for protection, was a young woman. She was peeping through dishevelled hair towards me, shaking with fear or pain. I could see that the door had probably hit her when it flew open. As it swung closed behind me, I pulled a window shutter open to get more light. I moved towards her, but she tried to crawl away from me. I had little experience of being gentle, for I had been in the company of rough men ever since I was abducted from my village. I had even less knowledge about how to treat a woman with feeling and sympathy. I reached forward and clumsily tried to help her get up from the floor. As I did so, she shook her head to clear hair from her face and turned to look at me. I was dumbstruck.

There was an apparition before me! The young woman's skin was the colour of honey or the light brown shade of autumn beech leaves before they are moistened by the dew. Her fall to the ground had caused her long jet-black tresses to be jumbled across the shawl round her shoulders. But her eyes, her eyes. Though they glistened with tears, I had never seen such beautiful dark eyes in my life.

In a flash, though still half crouching, she sprung to life. I saw a quick movement of the arm that had not been over her head and noticed the glint of metal. The scissors slashed across the side of my neck, just under my left ear. The sting of the cut shocked me and I fell backwards on-to a bed couch. I gasped for breath and struggled to remove the tension of my sword belt, throwing it to the ground. The girl was now standing, looking down at me. Her eyes betrayed that she was aghast at the effect of her attack. She dropped the scissors, put her hand to her mouth briefly, and then, seemingly having decided that something had to be done to atone for the wounding, pulled off her shawl and leant forward to wrap it around my neck in an effort to stench the copious blood oozing from the cut. Bizarrely, I found myself smiling at her in thanks. She returned a look with her lovely face contorted to show empathy for my pain.

I had little time to reflect on my misfortune and the fighting spirit of the girl. The door, which had swung closed, crashed open. There, with shoulders touching the door frame on both sides, stood the enormous bulk of Tor.

I shook my head to try to clear my mind as he strode towards where I was sitting. He grabbed me with both hands and threw me against the wall of the room. The blow stunned me, but I recovered quickly enough to avoid the punch that followed. I could see my knife on the belt I had discarded, in the corner of the room, but Tor stood between it and me. He grabbed me again and threw me through the open door out into the room we had first entered.

Mindless of the blood still flowing from my cut, I was desperate to protect the girl from Tor. I looked round the gloomy room. Where was Erik? There was no sign of him. I needed his help more than ever. The old man was gone too; only the woman, now sitting on the couch sobbing, was left. I had to do something. I could not let that bastard Tor violate the girl. I was already deeply infatuated by her. I could not bear to hear her screams. I frantically looked around in the half dark room for some weapon. My eye fell on a sheep's gut twine with a wooden handle at each end, on the table. It was a cheese cutter such as my mother used. The words of the old cook buzzed around my mind: "There are three chances to slay a man with little danger to the killer." One of them was "when he lies between a woman's legs and pleasures himself."

I grabbed the cheese cutter and quietly looked into the room. The girl was screaming, wriggling, and struggling as Tor held her down with one hand and vainly tried to undo his sword belt, to drop his trousers, with the other. I approached them from behind Tor's back and whipped the loop of the cheese cutter over his head, under his beard, and across his throat. Quickly swapping my hands over, I gripped the handles, crossing them behind his neck. I placed my knee in his back and pulled with all my strength. There was a loud gurgle as he desperately tried to get his fingers between the twine and his throat. Panicking, he tried to reach back to grab me, but the girl seized his arms and fought to stop him. He writhed and twisted to resist the two of us, trying to throw me off his back and detach the girl's hands from his wrists. The man had the strength of a giant but I gripped the handles with all my might, jerking the cord ever tighter by forcing my knee deeper into his back. Gradually, Tor's efforts to save himself diminished and then, quite suddenly, he slumped forward, falling on the girl. I held the grip for some time, lest he was feigning death, before dragging the heavy weight of the body off her and pushing it onto the floor.

She sat up and, though trembling with fright, leant forward to adjust the shawl round my bleeding neck, as the cloth had come loose in the fray. The wound was still stinging dreadfully. I was exhausted, as was she. I sat next to her on the couch shaking with shock, either from the cut or, more likely, from the relief of surviving the struggle with a more powerful man. We did not talk; indeed, at that time I did not know if we had language in common. I realise now that she was probably more in shock than me, but she was strong and showed more composure than I could muster. I tried to come to terms with the relief I felt to have killed my enemy and saved the girl, but at the same time I was elated to be near this beautiful young woman. We both sat on the bed with our backs to the wall, tears running down our faces.

The sun was reaching the open shutter and shining on the body of Tor when I got up and made to recover my belt and sword. I went out into the other room. Erik was sitting at the table, together with the old man, as well as the remnants of the food; both had wooden ale tankards in front of them. The old woman was busying about tidying and cleaning. She was no longer crying and seemed to have recovered from her previous terror.

"You took time, Ulf," mumbled Erik with a slurred voice. I was standing in a dark corner, and he had not noticed the blood on my tunic.

"No more than I needed. Where in the name of Odin were you when I looked for you?"

Erik was clearly very drunk. He picked up a piece of bread and, slapping the old man on the back, replied, "This is my new friend, who is called Egwine. He took me to the brew house and we tapped open an ale cask. He tells me that this is the first time he has tasted his master's ale!"

The lump of bread in his hand never reached his mouth. Looking behind me, his jaw dropped when he saw the dark girl come into the room. She rushed over to the old woman and threw her arms round her.

"My turn with her next," he said.

I now had my belt on. I drew my knife and raised it to within a hand span of Erik's nose and said quietly, "No one shall have her. You try and I will kill you."

Erik grinned. "As you will, Ulf. Perhaps Wilfrun has a daughter."

"You know the woman's name?"

"This village has been under the control of the Danes until the Saxons took it when she was a girl. She speaks some Norse."

"Ask her what my girl is called."

"You can ask her yourself."

The girl, still comforting the old lady, had her back to the two men. Wilfrun leant forward and said, "Her name is Hana. It means 'happiness' in her language. But what happiness does she get, or me?"

She seemed to have overcome her fear that we would kill her and was now unexpectedly forthright.

She continued, "It's bad enough serving a mean master. At least he makes penance in church, but to be forced to feed and care for you pagan Norse bastards is too much."

"She has a sharp tongue, Ulf," said Erik, grinning. "Don't listen. She is kind really. See, she has sewn up the tear in my shirt!"

"You'll want food too, I suppose," muttered Wilfrun.

"I told you. She is just like a mother, or grandmother."

Hana smiled at me as she took a wooden platter from a shelf. She deliberately touched my hand as she gave it to me before she started to ladle out some stew. She took some for herself and sat down next to me as I poured myself some ale. The drink had not wetted my lips before there was a sudden crash as the front door was forced open. There stood Botvig and Onäm.

"Well, the gods have blessed you two!" shouted Onäm.

"Food *and* women!" retorted Botvig.

"Any silver?" asked Onäm.

I spluttered, "We haven't looked."

The two of them roared with laughter.

"We have women and food at home, you don't need to cross an ocean to find them. We want silver to take home."

"But this is a little beauty," said Onäm, reaching towards Hana.

"She's mine, leave her," I said as I pushed my way between him and her.

"And these two are friendly, they are the miller's thralls," blurted Erik.

Onäm became very serious as he looked me in the eye and said, "That's not the way it is, Ulf. We warriors share the silver and the women."

"Not this one."

To my horror, I realised that I was pointing my knife at my uncle, my swordsmanship teacher, my mentor.

I lowered it and said, "I am sorry, Onäm, she is very special to me. Take all the silver you can find but leave her."

"Come have some ale!" added Erik, lifting his wooden tankard.

Onäm looked across at Botvig. They smiled and exchanged grins.

"How did you find us?" I asked.

"Botvig saw you leaving the village and walking this way."

"Was there good plunder in the village?"

"Not for us, Ulf. The place is too small, and we were too many. What happened to your neck?"

"Oh, it's nothing, just a cut. Will we sail today?"

"No, it's too late and there is total mayhem around the harbour and much needless slaughter."

"Then Erik and I will stay here for the night."

"If you want to save the women from the bloodlust of the other crews then you must send your new friends away quickly before more warriors find this place. I don't intend to be killed defending your young stupidity."

"We can take the old man and the women to the safety of their own people," said Erik.

"What madness has grasped you, Erik!? How do you think you will be received by the Saxons who lived here?" shouted Onäm angrily.

Erik was silent for a while and then said grumpily, "At least we won't have to eat and sleep on the ship tonight."

"One of our crew has already been here," I said.

"Yes? Where did he go?" asked Erik.

I nodded towards the small room and said, "He's in there."

The three men followed each other into the room to look.

There were exclamations of surprise, and then Onäm came out and looked at me with some admiration and said, "What in the name of the god of revenge did you do to him?"

"So it was he who nearly cut your throat," said Botvig, pointing to my neck.

I realised that the wound was still bleeding and wrapped Hana's shawl more tightly round it.

"He tried to take Hana," I said lamely.

Onäm leant towards me. "Best we keep this between ourselves, or it could go badly for you, Ulf. Killing a Geat warrior will not go down well with Toste. We'll say that a Saxon killed him."

"That's both of the bastards dead," Erik added gleefully, referring to the earlier killing of Agmunder.

"Come, we must hide the body," said Botvig.

Erik stood up and said, "I'll show you the way to the barn, we can hide his body there."

The ale cask lasted as long as the light, and so it was at dusk that Botvig and Onäm, in a merry mood, took leave of us and returned to the ship. Erik slept in the room where I had killed Tor. I slept in the miller's bed, but not alone.

The next morning, at Wilfrun's insistence, we fed the hens in the yard and the cows, before Erik and I put an ox into the shafts of an old cart and harnessed the animal to carry the old couple and Hana further inland and away from the risk of further visits from the Norsemen.

While we were working, they had put on thick coats and packed food in a basket to take with them. The women climbed onto the cart and we helped them with their few belongings. Finally, we lifted Egwine onto the back.

Shyly, I called to Hana, "I'll come back for you one day when there is peace in this land."

Hana nodded in a slight bow to me as she smiled coyly, and I could see that there were tears running down her face.

"Wilfrun, what is the name of this place?" I asked.

"Gippeswic," she answered.

Erik slapped the animal's rump and it slowly moved away, following the path inland. As it entered the tree lined track, both women turned to wave at us.

We went into the empty house and, remembering why we had come here in the first place, we searched around fruitlessly for anything of value that we could take.

By mid-morning we were on our way down the hill to the village. The looting and destruction was clear to see though from what men told us, it seemed that there was little of value to justify it. More than once warriors slapped me on the back and congratulated me on my wound. The blood-soaked shawl gave me honour among the men for it seemed that apart from the disappearance of one of our crew, there had been no other casualties in the very one-sided battle for the town.

That evening, there was no shortage of meat and beer, and as night fell there was much feasting and drunken ribaldry around camp fires in the wrecked village. As the drink flowed, Erik's voice got louder and louder and his tongue looser. I began to fear that he might blurt out about the women or, worse still, about the killing of Tor. Eventually, the risk was too great.

"Erik, come over here, over by the logs, I need to talk to you."

"Why, come join in the fun, Ulf, tell the story of your wound!"

"Yes, Ulf, come and tell us. Did you kill the bastard?" one of the revellers shouted. His voice was joined by others.

"It was nothing, I, I don't remember much, it happened too fast," I said.

"Was it a sword or a knife?" asked one.

"A knife I think."

"You think? Didn't you notice?" bellowed another.

There was loud guffawing, but it seemed that Erik might have grasped my difficulty for he put his arm around my bloody shoulder and, slurring his words, said, "What d'you want to talk about?"

"Come, let's go and sit on the logs over there."

We sat down and I hissed at him, "By the gods, Erik, guard your tongue, you'll have us both killed."

He was silent for a while and then said, "I wonder if they got to safety?"

I hesitated and responded, "I really hope so."

"Shall we go and look for them tomorrow?"

I was confused with a heady mix of infatuation and loss, but was not going to share my feelings with Erik. Instead, I growled at him, "You stupid sod, how long do you think we would survive if we ventured outside this town?"

With hurt feelings he said, "Then I shall find solace with ale," and left to return to his drinking companions.

As the campfires burned and the men got more and more rowdy, the captains met to discuss with the commander whither we should go next. When, later on, the word spread that the following day we would sail south to find richer towns, I realised with sorrow that my chances of ever seeing Hana again were remote.

CHAPTER 10

Northey Island, Maldon in the year 991

"How much longer are we to stay here, Ulf?" groaned Erik. "Why are you complaining, we eat well and there is little work to do while we are storm bound."

The Commander's plan for us to voyage south to find richer pickings had been delayed by strong contrary winds from the south-west. We had little to do apart from joining some of the raids inland, but it soon became clear that apart from gaining a plentiful supply of mutton and beef, there were few spoils to be had. The Saxons were well forewarned of our presence. The local people had fled and there was a strange emptiness in the region. The boredom began to cause outbursts of fighting between some of the other crews. Many old scores were settled, and despite dire warnings from the captains forbidding violence, some men were never to see home again and were left buried in the mud of Gippeswic. Eventually, the fleet departed, and we sailed south for two days before turning west in the late afternoon and being carried by the incoming tide along a wide waterway with the coast on both sides of the ships. We later learned that the river was called the Panta.

"Why are the ships in front stopping?" demanded Leif of one of his crew sitting near us. "Arvid, go up to the bow."

We all craned round to try to see what was happening, but the mass of the crew behind us and Dragon's high prow prevented us from seeing forward.

"The river is at an end, there is land ahead, an island!" shouted Arvid.

"What are they doing?" thundered Leif.

After a few moments Arvid shouted in response, "The ships are going round the island, there are just creeks on this side. They are beaching on the far shore."

"Ship oars!" commanded Leif as he turned the vessel so that he could get a better look at what was happening. Ahead of us was a low island with many mud flats quickly being covered by the incoming tide.

"All the ships are running up onto the shore, side by side," commented Erik.

He was right, and eventually, when there was space between the other manoeuvring ships, we too rowed forward round the north side of the island. A flock of geese, disturbed by our arrival, hurried to make way as Leif steered *Dragon* in towards the land. Soon, we felt the hull slow down as it was seized by the mud in the shallow water. Later, when the tide was higher, we were able to get the bow up against the low grass crested ridge of the shore. We became wedged in between many other ships, and we could climb directly onto the land from the bow.

"*Dragon* crew, wait on the shore in front of the ship!" bellowed Leif.

We did as we were ordered and milled around with our ship mates, surveying our surroundings. Other crews had also gathered in front of their ships, awaiting orders.

"Look there's Tryggvason's ship, and there is Toste!" shouted Erik, trying to make himself heard over the babble of conversation.

The two commanders had raised their standards by their ships so that they could be identified among the mass of men.

"Wait here for orders. Gather wood and start a fire so that we can eat, there may soon be a battle!" boomed Captain Leif as he hurriedly departed in the direction of Tryggvason's banner.

"I see what he means, Erik. Look over there."

"Where?"

"You see, over by that village, armed men are riding towards us."

"But they can't get over the water to us, can they?"

"No, the water is too deep."

We stood watching the mounted warriors on the other side of the river. They were followed by columns of marching men. Then we lost sight of them as they were obscured by the only hill on the island.

"We can't bring them to battle unless they cross to us, or we cross to them," said Botvig, who was standing by my side.

I became aware of a noise. Gradually, the sound of men shouting got louder and louder. The Saxons were jeering at us, for they knew the difficult situation we were in. Soon the Norsemen began to respond with whoops, yells, and curses, and before long the few geese that were left had all taken to the air in fright.

"I think our swords will taste blood, Saxon blood, before long," said Onäm.

"If we can get at them," replied Botvig.

Our crew all joined in the shouting, and we competed with the neighbouring crews to produce the most gross insults and profanities directed at the Saxons.

"Save your breath. It's too late in the day for a battle, we can kill more if we can see them in day light," growled Wolve.

After a while the crescendo of shouting declined, and we set about building a cooking fire.

"We give battle in the morning!" shouted Leif breathlessly as he hurried towards us. "The crews must take turns at guarding the ships during the night, for the fear is that the Saxons might try to burn them."

After we had eaten, men gathered round campfires to work by the light of the flames. The night air was alive with the rasp of weapons being sharpened.

I was aware that Onäm was watching as I ran the stone back and forth along the edge of my sword. Glancing around to see that no one was within earshot, he leant forward to me and said, "Ulf, I kept my word about the way Tor died. Now I want you to repay the debt."

"How?"

"When I fought Wolve in the contest, I should have killed him, though it would have been difficult with the weapons we used. I knew though that I should not try to do so because we wanted to improve our relationship with the Geats. I also knew that he would be humiliated if he survived. He lost some honour."

"And so what do you want me to do?"

"Like any man who has been humiliated he bears a grudge against the source of his humiliation."

"And you think he may try to kill you during the battle?"

"Exactly. As you will see, in the frantic heat of a battle when swords swing wildly, shields push against shields, and spears fly, it is easy for a man to settle an old score without being noticed."

"That is what Old Cook once foretold."

"I want you to stay behind me and warn me if you see Wolve sneaking too close."

"I will." I hesitated for a moment and then said, "Do you know if the Saxons are good fighters?"

There was a long silence, and then my uncle asked, "Are you worried about tomorrow?"

I was surprised by his question. To show fear would be shameful, but the truth was that even the most hardened warrior has an anxious night before a battle, though few would admit it.

"No, no not really, but I want to live to take my fortune home."

"You have to find the fortune first," said Onäm, laughing.

"Oh, I will. If the king of this country sends such an army against us, he must have great wealth to protect."

"True, but if you die here it will be an honourable warrior's death."

"Who talks of death?" The voice of Leif was unmistakable.

"It should be the Saxons who talk of death, for I will account for many of them on the morrow," said Erik.

"How many men have they?" Onäm asked Leif.

"Tryggvason thinks that they have no more than us, about three thousand men. But he says that many of them will be from the fyrd, untrained farmers who must fight to serve their lord."

"Then we will scythe them like they scythe corn," interjected Wolve.

The next morning the ships' crews were lined up in rows on the slope of the hill on the island, facing the Saxon army. The height gave us a very good view of what was happening on the shore. We were surprised to see that today none of the men on the other side of the river were mounted, and there was no sign of the fine war horses we had seen yesterday.

"Where are the horses?" I asked of no one in particular.

"Perhaps they want to spare them from our spears," ventured one voice.

"No, I have fought Saxons before. They send the horses away so that their owners can't be tempted to flee the battle if things go badly," said another.

We all considered this answer as we waited for some decision to be made about how we could reach our enemy. Finally, we saw Olaf Tryggvason walk to the water's edge, but as he did so, our attention was drawn to the fact that as the tide water receded, a very narrow strip of land began to appear between the island and the mainland. There was a causeway!

Then we noticed a very tall figure in a fine cloak, wearing a magnificent gold helmet, striding to the water's edge in front of the Saxons.

Tryggvason spoke first. He shouted across the river, "How is this place named, my lord?"

A man stood beside the Saxon nobleman, obviously translating what had been spoken.

"This is the town of Maeldun. I am Earl Byrhtnoth and I command you to return whence you came."

This statement was translated for Olaf Tryggvason and those who heard it started to laugh and jeer at the Saxon earl.

The Norse commander raised his hand to silence his followers.

"Yes, we will leave. We will leave on payment of gold and armour."

There was a pause and then the earl shouted across the water, "Yes, we will pay you. We will pay you with spear tips and sword blades."

By this time, the causeway linking the island with the mainland was clear for all to see. As we watched, our commander sent a file of men to cross the narrow strip. As they tried to do so they were cut down by a hail of Saxon arrows and their bodies lay strewn in the mud.

We watched with anticipation as our commanders conferred. Then Tryggvason strode to the shore again, seemingly unafraid of the chance that he might become the target of a Saxon arrow.

"Is the earl so cowardly that he does not dare to do battle, man to man? Are his men so craven that they act like dogs holding a bear at bay, barking but not biting?"

There was a pause as this was translated to the earl. We all studied him to see his response. He was a huge man, by far the tallest among those warriors around him.

His message was shouted across the mud by his interpreter, "You Norsemen are brave enough when you raid defenceless villages and the houses of God. Come, come to our shore and face a bolder enemy. By nightfall your ships will not be needed, for there will be none left to row them!"

As the Saxon force began to draw back from the shore and form up in battle lines further inland, our men started to file across the causeway and organise themselves parallel to the Saxons.

Tryggvason, surrounded by his house carls and his two scalds, men who would later record the battle and tell of our valour, formed up in the centre of the front line. He kept glancing around at the assembling men, waving at some and pointing which way they should deploy. We were directed to form up on his right side. The men who usually used heavy, long-handled axes to stop charging cavalry horses were ordered to arm themselves with short axes and spears for close combat.

It was easy for us to distinguish between the men of the Saxon fyrd and the warriors of the earl's house carls. The farmers were bowmen in the first two ranks. Here and there officers were shouting orders and moving groups of bowmen, axemen, and warriors into position.

There was a lot of shouting and exchanging of insults, though we could not understand what was said and they could probably not comprehend the curses we were hurling at them. The noise slowly died down until, apart from the occasional order barked by officers, there was a silence, a deathly silence.

A loud voice somewhere in the Saxon ranks, made an exclamation. We saw the bowmen immediately draw their bows. There was a great "whoosh" as the first flight of arrows were loosed by the Saxons. Looking up, we could see the arrows coming towards us. We steeled ourselves for the inevitable effect, holding up shields to protect ourselves as much as possible. There were curses, grunts, and some screams, and all along our front line, men dropped to the ground or to their knees.

As the bowmen reloaded, Tryggvason rushed forward, sword in hand, surrounded by his best men, one carrying his banner. A roar went up from the charging Norsemen.

"Run forward, Ulf, we're not staying here to give the Saxons target practice!" shouted Onäm.

The Norse charged and the distance between the two armies closed quickly as the Saxons surged forward too. The men of the fyrd, with no protective armour or shields, abandoned their bows and inflicted whatever injuries they could with their knives, reaphooks, and short axes as they moved back to be replaced by the seasoned, well-armed soldiers. Any fear I had had disappeared and was replaced by rage as I saw comrades being cut down in front of me. In a very short time, we were shield-to-shield with the warriors. The crescendo of cheering and whooping from both sides was quickly replaced by cursing and screaming as men were wounded and maimed. There was a dreadful chorus of the dull thumping of swords on shields. We picked our way over bodies, helmets, and equipment to get at the enemy. I swung and slashed my sword trying to find a weak spot in the defence of the men in front of me, a chink of flesh not covered by a shield or chain mail. These were not the farmers we had been told about; these were skilled warriors.

I ducked as a sturdy man ahead of me with a long drooping blonde moustache made a massive swing at neck height. His sword caught Arvid's shoulder and severed his arm almost straight through. While the Saxon stretched up to extricate his sword, I saw that his short mail shirt lifted, exposing his lower stomach. I lunged at him and plunged my weapon into his belly. As he fell backwards, I saw his angered companion raise his sword over my head, but as he did so a spear pierced his throat. I glanced behind and saw Erik grinning at me. Behind him, I noticed the bulk of Wolve slashing his way through the confusion of fighters, his blue and white shield held high. I had forgotten what Onäm had asked me to do!

Holding men at bay as best I could, I looked for him.

"Erik, can you see Onäm!?" I shouted, hoping that my tall friend might see more than me.

"Over there!" He pointed, narrowly avoiding a spear thrown at him.

I followed the direction of his arm and saw my uncle in the thick of a double combat with two Saxons, avoiding them with his characteristic weaving and ducking. Wolve was almost behind him.

I fought my way sideways, slipping on the blood-soaked grass and parrying the blows of swords with my shield.

As I came up behind Wolve, I saw that he had taken his knife out of the sheath with his left hand. He was stalking Onäm, who was now directly in front of him. Space was too limited by the weight of fighters around me to allow me to swing my sword at him. I grabbed my knife, but the chain mail hanging from the back of his helmet protected his neck. In desperation, I swung the knife low into his unprotected left thigh.

"Arghh!" screamed Wolve as the pain hit him.

He swivelled round and saw me, knife in my left hand, behind him. He forgot any thought of the enemy behind him and lunged at me with his knife. As he did so, Erik's spear pierced his armour and sank into his chest.

The battle and the awful slaughter of friend and foe continued for a long time. We were desperate for an indication that we were overcoming the enemy, for they seemed to be fighting as hard as ever. The carnage was such that we stood on dead warriors as we fought; there was no space left on the red grass. Then, suddenly, there was a roar of many voices, a sound much louder than the constant cacophony of the shouts and screams of the warriors; something had happened. Something important. The fighting continued but gradually the numbers in front of us began to dwindle. Then we saw that some of the Saxons, mainly the men of the fyrd, were turning and leaving the field. Some had even found horses and were mounting to ride off.

"Byrhtnoth is dead!" shouted some of the Norse warriors. We tried to see whether the Saxon commander's standard was still planted on the field to our left. Between the heaving bodies of those still fighting we got an occasional glimpse of the flag. It was still flying.

Then the fighting began to become more sporadic. It was clear that an increasing number of those Saxons who had survived were now fleeing. Soon we could see a battle raging around the earl's standard. About twenty Saxons were valiantly trying to stave off the Norse warriors encircling them. It was clear that they were high ranking soldiers. Tryggvason was there too, and we watched as he raised his sword in the air and, shouting at the top of his voice, commanded his warriors to stop attacking the embattled knot of Saxons. We who had survived the battle moved closer to see what was to happen.

"You Saxons have your dead commander at your feet, a spear through his chest. You have fought valiantly as true warriors. The field is ours, but you may depart and take the news of my victory to your king."

The message was interpreted to the Saxons. There was a deep silence among the Norse as the dead earl's closest and best warriors conferred. They said nothing to our commander but formed a circle around their dead leader. Each of them faced outwards and, in defiance, raised their swords at those surrounding them.

"These are brave men, great warriors, men worthy of a place in Valhalla." I recognised Onäm's voice behind me.

"But they have the chance to live," said Erik.

"No, they have the chance to die an honourable death," answered Onäm solemnly.

Olaf Tryggvason once more held his sword above his head, then he lowered it to signify that the battle should recommence. Many of the Norse rushed forward to seize the chance to kill the heroic Saxons and the affair was soon over.

"The legend of those Saxons will last a thousand years. They sought to avenge their noble leader," reflected Onäm. Then he paused and asked, "Have you seen Wolve?"

I looked round me to see that I was not to be overheard and then said, "Yes, you were right. He died fighting, but his killer was not a Saxon."

"Then you are no longer in my debt, Ulf."

Though we were elated, we were all very tired. We stood wearily scanning the scene around us. Norsemen and Saxons lay in tangled heaps. Some were still alive, and the sound of the roar of voices in victory after the recent slaughter of the last Saxons had given way to the moaning, wailing, and screaming of the near dead.

"Ulf, we have survived a battle such as I have never seen before. We were very lucky that the farmers fled, for it left the Saxon warriors outnumbered. It would have otherwise been a very close thing for us."

With Onäm's words echoing in my mind we set about killing the worst wounded Saxons who were sitting, kneeling in prayer, or lying, littered around the bloody field. As we did so we plundered the bodies for anything of value. The spoils were good, and as we returned to our ships, supporting those of our own who were wounded, I was satisfied to feel the weight of the silver in my money belt, the pull on my neck of a heavy Saxon necklace, and the cold sensation on my wrist from a bracelet.

CHAPTER 11

It was first when we returned on our thwarts on the ship that the full extent of the cost of our victory became clear. Captain Leif stood in the stern, blood dripping from the chain mail sleeve on his left arm.

"Here, come, lad, help me drag this off," he said, beckoning to me.

He sat on his stool while I gingerly tried to pull the mail over his head without causing further damage to his arm. He took a sharp intake of breath as I peeled the sleeve off. He had an open wound on his forearm, probably from a spear. He wiped the blood away and I helped him to bind a cloth over the gash. He stood up and looked down the length of the ship.

"We will need to find slaves to row with us if we are ever to return to our land," he muttered.

I turned to look. The scene was appalling. Many thwarts were empty; on some, men sat with their heads bowed, exhausted. Others were binding cuts and lacerations.

I turned to Erik and said, "Have you seen Botvig?"

He stood up and climbed onto his bench to get a better look.

"No, when did you last see him?"

"Not since the beginning of the battle."

"He must be dead. Just three of us left from Gnir's army now."

The next day we found Botvig's body; his face having been split by a sword slash, he was barely recognisable. His own sword was still under his body.

"Take it, Erik, Botvig no longer needs it, and it is a good Frankish one," said Onäm.

"Will you teach me to use it?"

"That I will, but first we have a job to do. We must bury our old comrade."

"Let's find his knife and perhaps he has some silver," said Erik.

"Leave the knife with him, and if he has silver, let him take it with him to the next world as he will surely be admitted by the Valkyries," answered Onäm.

Our work done, we walked around the field and watched as Saxon women and boys, who had been permitted free passage by Tryggvason, searched for their husbands and fathers. Bodies were being loaded on carts, to the wailing of relatives. At the site of the last stand of the Saxon warriors, a group of shaven-headed men in black cloaks were tending to the headless body of Earl Byrhtnoth. The corpse had been awfully mutilated even after his death.

It was on the second day after the battle that word spread that we were to remain on the island to await the arrival of a deputation from the English king. Further, that we were not to plunder the town of Maeldun, but instead to wait for Tryggvason to negotiate with the Saxons. Meanwhile, we were supplied with cattle and flour by the inhabitants of the town.

It was several days before a force of mounted Saxon warriors arrived, escorting a nobleman in fine clothes. We later learnt that he was leader of the Saxon's religion, Archbishop Siric. A tent had been set up on the grass across the water, and we crowded on the hill to watch Tryggvason greet the visitors before showing the nobleman into the tent.

"We are to be paid in silver to leave these shores! The Saxons are to pay Danegeld."

Leif's voice boomed down the ship as he took up his position in the stern after returning from a conference with the other captains and the commanders.

There was a loud cheer from the depleted crew, and it was echoed from other ships as the agreement was announced through the fleet.

"How much?" came a shout from behind me.

"Ten thousand pounds of Saxon silver," Leif answered.

"How much is that?" called another voice.

The captain hesitated for a moment and then shouted, "About the weight of seven or eight men."

When the cheers had died down, I recognised Onäm's voice calling out, "And how is it to be shared?"

"Leif Tryggvason and Toste will keep one thousand pounds each, the captains get thirty pounds each, and every warrior will get almost 3 pounds."

"What is three pounds?" asked Erik.

"The weight of a plump chicken, my lad, worth about thirty-six aurar."

"When do we get it?"

"Tryggvason and Toste are to sail to the great Saxon harbour up the next river, with ten ships to escort them. They will collect the silver there and return it to us here."

It was another two weeks before our commanders returned with their laden ships and almost as long for the silver to be shared out. The process of distributing the silver was beset with problems. While some of the silver was in coins, each one with a picture of the head of the Saxon king, Ethelred, much of it was made up of silver jewellery and ornaments. These had to be cut and carefully weighed.

There were more than two thousand men, some badly wounded, and we all wanted our fair share. The laden ships had berthed in the small harbour at Maeldun, and on the day they had arrived, the crews of all the waiting vessels had rushed there. We all massed around the boats, jostling to get nearest to the fortune. Like everyone else, I wanted to be certain that there was enough to ensure that I got what was my right.

"Move back, clear a way!" shouted Tryggvason, standing on the stern of his mighty ship. He sent his fully armed housecarls, his personal retinue, ashore to threaten those nearest the vessels and force a path for the captains of the fleet to go on board to discuss how every man would be rewarded.

"How are they going to quell the will of each of this mob to get their share first?" shouted Onäm to us.

"Come, let's move back, this is getting very ugly," I commented.

Brawls had broken out in some parts of the crowd and bloodshed was inevitable.

"Yes, after surviving the battle it would indeed be tragic to die waiting for our reward," said
Onäm.

It seemed that many others were of the same mind, and the surging of the clamouring crowd eased as others turned and spread out a distance behind the troublemakers. We climbed onto the back of a cart and watched while the captains boarded the flag ship.

"What can they be talking about all this time?" moaned Erik.

"Look, they are beginning to come ashore," said Onäm.

The captains made their way through the crowds towards where we were standing. As they did so, their crews disentangled themselves from the mass of men and followed them.

"Over there!" shouted Leif as he pointed towards a giant oak tree.

We made our way towards the tree, passing many others going in different directions to join their captains.

"The earl wishes me to tell you that you must be patient!" he shouted.

There were groans from several of the crew.

"Haven't we been patient long enough?" called one.

"Any more complaints and I will ensure that you will be last to get your silver," the captain

retorted.

There were no more comments.

"A scribe on the flagship has noted the names of every vessel. We have drawn lots to decide the order that the booty will be handed out to crew members. The Dragon will be seventeenth. For those of you who never learned to count, it looks like this."

He held up first all his fingers, and then one hand showing all the fingers, and on his other, two.

"You should each make a bag from cloth for your share to be put in. There is plenty of cloth left on the battlefield. The dead won't be needing it."

And so it was that we queued two days later, waiting for our bags to be filled and the contents

carefully weighed. As we walked back to our ship Onäm said, "Now our problems begin."

"How do you mean?" I asked.

"We have to get this fortune home. We are surrounded by violent men, many of whom would cut your throat for a silver coin, and we have many."

There were no safe places on a ship to hide valuables, so we, like hundreds of others, carried our silver round with us. Under the watchful eye of Leif, on the ship we were safe, but on land there was much thieving. Some of the men chose to have their silver melted down into "ankle money." Strips of their silver were bent into shape so that they could be worn round their ankles and hidden by their boots, safe from thieves on the ships or, when they got home, from robbers.

Tales abounded of men who had lost silver in bouts of drinking, but most often it was gambling that stole many fortunes. We urged Captain Leif to leave as soon as possible, but he had to wait. Tryggvason needed the army stay until he was certain there would be no reprisal attack from the Saxons

The green leaves on the trees were beginning to change colour by the time we were given permission to sail. Before doing so, we raided the town and took Saxon slaves. Seven of them were chained to the benches on the *Dragon* until we were sufficiently far from land for there to be no risk of them leaping into the sea and swimming ashore. We now had a full crew. Our time in Aenglandi had taught us that the wind blew most steadily in the direction we were to travel, and soon after we set off, the great unreefed sail carried us quickly away from the land.

"We have wealth, but no women, Ulf," complained Erik as we sat watching the sunset over the increasingly distant coast of the land of the Saxons.

"I have wealth; I can find a new woman."

"You lie, Ulf. Your woman is there," he said, pointing at the horizon.

I was taken aback; Erik was not usually so perceptive. I lapsed into silence and closed my eyes to try to picture her sweet face and those dark eyes. The image was well preserved in my imagination, as was my infatuation. I knew that one day I would return.

Other ships left Maeldun at the same time as us, all the crews eager to be home before the onset of late autumn and the risk of bad weather both at sea and on land. Many of the men were from places far from our ships' destination, the Geat fortress, and they had further journeys to make when we arrived there. As indeed we had. All of us, aware of the dangers ahead, were anxious to reach our homes with our silver fortunes. Some ships were slower than ours, but several were faster, and we soon lost sight of them at sea.

News of the return of the fleet had obviously been spread at the fortress by those who arrived ahead of us. Many people waiting in the harbour had heard the sensational story of the battle and, in particular, the wealth carried by the impending arrivals. The latter was bound to attract every villain in the region to exact a share of the victors' spoils.

"Erik, Ulf, be careful. As soon as we get ashore, we must find a hostelry where we can stay safely until we find passage on a vessel going north."

"But just look at the rows of street vendors," I said, pointing at the line of colourful stalls on the quayside. Despite the drizzle, the cobbled street was packed with tradespeople. Even before willing hands ashore had grabbed our lines, some sellers surged forward to the side of the ship, trying to attract our attention. They held up bread, platters of fish, apples, jugs of ale, and all manner of clothing and footwear.

We made fast, helped to stow the sail, and then washed down and scrubbed the area round our thwarts, trying to ignore the shouts of those vying to sell their wares.

"Keep your weapons ready, lads. There are bound to be rogues in this crowd, keen to cheat and rob us," said Onäm.

After buckling on our sword belts under our raincoats, we tied up our few belongings in bundles and then went round the ship saying goodbye to those of the crew we counted as friends and ignoring those we did not. Finally, we returned to our thwarts to collect our shields from the side of the ship and to take leave of Captain Leif.

In an uncharacteristically quiet voice, Leif said, "How old are you boys?"

Erik looked at me and asked, "Do you know, Ulf?"

"Not really, I try to work out how many winters I was at Aros, for I know that I had been through about twelve before we went there."

"You must have been five years at Gnid's place," said Onäm.

"So, by now you must have lived through eighteen winters," commented the captain.

"How many's that?" asked Erik.

The captain held up his fingers twice to show Erik.

"Why do you ask, Leif?"

"Well, Onäm, these lads have survived such a battle as scalds will tell of for many generations. These two will be able to tell their children, and their children's children, and them in their turn that come after, of the honour of the Norsemen and how they made history in Maeldun."

"Do you think we have bled the Saxons of all the silver in their country?" I asked.

"No, not by a long way. I have no doubt that *Dragon* will be sailing that way again 'ere many winters have passed," he answered.

"Then perhaps we may meet again," said Erik.

"Indeed, we might," he answered.

"I don't think so, Captain, for I have other ideas for the future," I added.

The captain laughed and said, "I have heard that said before by those who have voyaged with me many times. Farewell, and be careful ashore."

I got up courage, and, trying to sound as confident as I could, pointed at a group of bemused men still sitting on their thwarts and asked, "What will happen to the Saxon captives?"

The captain roared with laughter, as did Onäm.

"What do you think, boy? I shall sell them. They are strong men; they'll fetch a good price."

"Then, Captain, will you sell one to me?"

"To you, Ulf? Why?

"I need a thrall to help with the work I am going to do."

I could not avoid noticing the surprise on my uncle's face and the gasp from Erik.

"The going price for a healthy man is ten auror of silver."

I delved into the bag on my belt, where I was keeping some of my silver, and retrieved most of the coins.

"Which one do you want?"

"That one, the man who calls himself 'Elfgar.'"

I had noticed the man during our voyage. When we were not rowing, he always kept himself busy, seeking out small jobs to do. He was tall and well built. A man who would be useful for the heavy tasks I had planned.

"A good choice, lad." Raising his voice, he shouted towards the stern, "Elfgar, come here!"

The Saxon, got up, left his place and walked towards the stern.

I had noticed before that when Leif had trouble communicating with those who did not speak Norse well, he always raised his voice, in the belief that this would help them understand.

In his open palm he held up the coins I had given him, pointed to me, and then to himself and said loudly, "Ulf has paid me for you. You must go with him."

Elfgar looked at me quizzically. I think he understood, but was just shocked that his master-to-be was one so young.

All of the Saxons had taken over the belongings of the previous, now dead, occupants of the thwarts they sat on. So, grabbing hold of my raincoat to illustrate what he meant and pointing at Elfgard's thwart, he said, "Get your coat."

As we climbed over the gunnel of the ship and onto the quay, Onäm said, "I don't know what you have in mind, boy, but your thrall has cost you almost a fourth part of the silver you have. Now you have to pay for your thrall's bed and food."

"I will," I answered.

We pushed our way through the throng of vendors, each with our shields strapped on our backs and one hand on the hilt of the knives we carried in our belts. Several people, mainly men, called out, "Place to sleep!" and we stopped several times to look them over with the assumption that the appearance of the caller would indicate the quality of the accommodation being offered. Onäm asked several men the price for a space for four to spend the night and eventually said, "Let's try this one. We must make a decision before more ships come in, there will be hundreds more looking for a bed and that will make the price go up."

We followed the man along the quay and through several narrow streets. Eventually, he stopped and pointed to a door, and we followed him in. He threw open a window shutter and enough light came through for us to see a hearth in the centre of the room and space for several to sleep on the rush covered floor around it. The air coming through the window eased the smell of the piss bucket in the corner of the room. He went over to it, picked it up, and cast the contents out of the window.

"What do you think, lads?" asked Onäm, turning away from the landlord.

"Let's take it for one night and then decide tomorrow if we stay longer," I suggested.

And so it was agreed that we should make the place our temporary home, perhaps until we could find a ship to take us north. We paid for the night and asked for firewood to be brought to us.

"We must go out to get food, but we can't walk around the town carrying our silver," said Onäm.

"Erik and I can stay here with your money bag while you go out. Take Elfgar with you," I suggested.

"That would give me the chance to ask around to see if there are any ships going to Svealand. Put the lock on the door while I am away."

This was agreed, and Eric and I set about lighting the fire to dry out our clothes. We were both asleep by the fire when we were woken by banging on the door. The pair had returned, laden with bread, meat, and ale. Onäm told us the good news, that there was a trading vessel going to Svealand in two days, on which we could make a passage.

"So, we have two nights to spend in this hovel," I said.

"Yes, we must be careful, there are a lot of devious looking men swarming around the streets, obviously looking to find their fortunes."

"But Erik and I must go out some time, we can't stay in here for two days."

"And I'm not going to! I want to see the town," said Erik in a belligerent way.

Onäm calmed the situation by spreading the food on the rush mat. He knew that the sight of it would quieten Erik.

"Come on, let's eat."

Unfortunately, the ale had the opposite effect.

"I'm going out now and no one is going to stop me," said Erik.

Onäm gave an exasperated sigh.

"Don't be stupid. A few ales and alone you'll be an easy target for a robber."

"Then let Ulf go with me."

Onäm was silent for a moment, and though seething with anger, he realised that there was no point in arguing further.

"Ulf, you go with him and make sure he is careful. Leave your swords, just take your knives."

"What about Elfgar?" I asked.

"Yes, you're right. I must make sure he doesn't cut my throat if I doze off. All this silver is a big temptation. Help me tie his hands."

Elfgar was not pleased that we showed such mistrust, but he seemed to understand why we did it.

Onäm put his hand on my shoulder and said, "Remember the darkness hides evil that would be seen in daylight. Be careful."

Assuring Onäm that we could take care of ourselves, we put on our rain jackets and left the house. The wet cobbles were glistening with the reflection of lanterns hung outside some houses. As we walked, we looked in through the open shutters of the small houses, seeing that there was much merriment: men singing, women laughing, banter, and some children screaming. In some cases, the celebrations had spilled out into the street and men and women, arms entwined, swayed back and forth, rocking, unbalanced by the quantity of ale they had drunk. I was shocked that here and there the casualties of the untamed consumption of drink had fallen, either staring at the stars or faces into the mud. It was clear that many hundreds more crewmen had arrived at the harbour during the afternoon.

"Why are you fine young men in a hurry?" shouted a woman to us as we sauntered past a crowd outside a particularly large house.

"Ain't you thirsty, lads?" shouted another as she beckoned us to join the crowd.

"Come on, Erik," I said. "Let's go."

One of the women seized the corner of his jacket and pulled him into the throng.

"It's all right, Ulf, we'll have just one ale and then move on."

I saw that there was no point in arguing. Other people nearby were making jokes about us.

"Got a boat to catch?"

"Want to ask your mother first?"

A man appeared with a jug of ale and two tankards, which he proceeded to fill.

The company we found ourselves in seemed convivial and friendly enough, and the conversation was good. Most had tales to tell of their time in Aenglandi and the voyage home. There was an atmosphere of fun, and I could see that Erik, who had moved deeper into the crowd, was having a good time.

After a while, conscious of Onäm's words, I shouted to Erik, "Come on, we must move on."

"You can if you like, but I'll stay here a while. Where are you going?"

"I'll go down to the quay to see if any of our shipmates are down there by the ship."

"I'll come down later."

I hurried on towards the quay, hoping that some of my shipmates might be around the *Dragon*. As I edged through a narrow passageway, I felt a hand take hold of shoulder. Grabbing the hilt of my knife, I turned. In the murky light I saw that a woman had seized my jacket.

"What do you want?" I demanded.

"No, my beauty, what do you want?"

I kept walking, but she held on and dragged behind me. I turned a corner and in front of me was a flaming torch. I turned again. Now I could see that the woman was young. She was dressed in a flimsy shift, more like bed wear. Her hair was tousled as if she had been in a high wind.

"Let go!" I demanded.

"You want that? You don't like me?

"What do you want of me?"

She moved forward and dropped her hand from my jacket to my crotch. The effect was instantaneous. I was on fire with desire. She pulled me back into the dark passage we had just passed and into an alcove formed by the crossed timbers at the corner of a house.

"Let go of your knife, my lovelie, and caress me."

I dropped my hands and pulled her towards me. She fiddled with my belt.

A scuffling sound behind alerted me too late. There was the sound of something moving fast through the air. I was conscious of a weight hitting my head, perhaps a cudgel. While fighting to resist the dimming of my brain, there was a second blow.

I don't know how long I was unconscious, but at some time I must have been pushed or pulled off the ground to a sitting position in the alcove, for it was so I found myself when I flitted in and out of reality. From time to time, I was aware of the ribaldry in the street and people shouting as they passed. But no one helped. Of course, they thought that I was drunk.

It was beginning to get light when I felt myself being lifted by hands under my armpits and heard a familiar voice.

"Ulf, can you not be trusted!?" demanded Onäm. "I have searched for you most of the night."

He continued, "That Erik loves the ale, we know, but I see you have the same weakness!"

"No, no it was not drink," I protested.

As he stood me up, my trousers fell down.

"And you have lost your belt and with it your knife and your purse. Curse you, fool! Now you have no silver. Nothing to show for the blooding of your sword and the misery of our voyage."

Unsteadily, I bent down to pull up my trousers, and as I did so, my uncle saw the bloody tangle of hair on the top of my head.

"By the gods, what happened to you?"

I was not inclined to mention the girl, for I was ashamed of my stupidity.

"I was attacked and robbed. Don't you see?"

"Where?"

"Here, just here. I was cudgelled and my belt stolen."

Onäm moderated his tone and said, "You are lucky your own knife was not used on you."

"Pox on the rogues, I have had that knife since we were with Gnir."

I was now standing with more certainty; nevertheless I was grateful for Onäm's hand gripping my arm as, with him, I stumbled towards our lodgings, one hand holding up my trousers.

Onäm banged on the door of the house and shouted, "Erik, unlock the door!"

We heard the creak of the wooden latch being lifted and pushed the door open.

"I found him, the young fool got robbed and he's lost his silver."

I started to laugh.

"Has the cudgel addled his brain?" said my rescuer angrily.

Erik began laughing too, increasing Onäm's annoyance.

"Tell him, Ulf."

I sat down on a stool and struggled to pull off one of my boots. I was still quite shaky, and the effort was difficult. Erik stepped over to help.

Revealing my foot, I pulled up my trouser leg slightly. Though in the dull light, the metal band round my ankle did not shine, there was no doubt that it was silver.

Onäm looked on, open mouthed. "When did you do that?"

"When the blacksmith came round to the ships to melt down coins and silver valuables. Lots of men did this, but we all kept it secret for fear that if we were robbed, the attacker would have to cut off a foot to get the silver."

"I thought he was stupid because he had to pay an aura to get it done," said Erik.

"I only had a few coins in my purse when I went out last night," I added.

There was a long period of silence while Onäm allowed his mood to change from one of anger to sympathy with a tinge of admiration.

"Elfgar, go to the pump and get water. I must bathe Ulf's head, then we will go out together, fully armed, to find a leather merchant where Ulf can buy a new belt and purse."

"I need a knife too."

"Yes, but you have no coins and you do not wish us to cut your foot off."

"I'll lend him some of my silver," said Erik.

Later, we put our belongings into packs on our backs and our jackets on over them to stop thieves. Erik and Onäm had their silver inside theirs.

After we had found a leather merchant and had a belt made, we followed directions he had given us to find an arms smith.

We smelt the smoke of his hearth and heard the clanging of metal on metal before we rounded a corner in a street of badly built hovels. The smithy was set apart from other buildings because of the fire risk. The open sided building was attached to a hut. When we approached it, the smith was shaping a glowing length of iron. Sparks flew as he worked. Near to him a boy knelt on the ground pumping hand bellows, the spout of which led to an airway under the roaring fire.

The smith noticed our approach but did not stop work. We stood watching.

The glow of the iron dulled, and he thrust it into a barrel of water, raising a column of steam. Putting the metal down onto his anvil, he turned to us. He looked us up and down and then said, "I see you have swords already, so what do you want?"

Onäm drew his knife from his belt and held it up. "We need a knife for my companion." He beckoned to me.

The smith stepped towards him. Onäm turned the handle towards the smith and handed over the knife. The smith closely inspected the blade.

"You're Svea, aren't you?" he growled.

We had forgotten the discrimination we had suffered a year before.

"Why? Don't you sell to our kind?" said Onäm aggressively.

"Oh yes, I sell to anyone who has silver. I mention it because I can see the quality of your knife is such that you won't find here."

"Why not?"

"Because the Svear keep all the best iron for themselves. We have no iron in this region, we must buy from the north lands."

"And the Svea smiths keep the best?"

"Yes, and there is a shortage here. Most of my stock was used arming Toste's men."

"So can you make a knife? We are in a hurry, for we sail tomorrow.

"No, I need more time. It would be better for you to go to the harbour and buy from the money lender."

"Money lender?"

"Yes, drunkards, thieves, and destitute people sell their goods for silver."

"Where is this place?"

"At the west end of the harbour, a house facing the sea. There are usually some carts by the side of it. On good days like today, the shutters are open, and you can see the things they have for sale."

As we walked towards the harbour, Onäm said, "How strange that there is a shortage of iron in Geat country. I never heard of this in Aros."

We found the house of the money lender quite easily. There was a small crowd milling around outside; we pushed past them and stood at an open shutter, inside of which we could see stacks of different things: helmets, clothes, pots, pans, horse harnesses, and much more.

"Yes, Captain," the vendor said to Onäm, who was clearly the oldest of us. The overweight tradesman waddled up to the shutter and grinned.

"You buying or selling?"

Onäm once more took out his knife. He handed it to the merchant.

"Look at this. I want a knife like it."

The man looked carefully at the blade and grinned as he said, "I could give you a good price for this."

The Svear warrior's patience snapped.

With a raised voice he said, "I don't want to sell, I want to buy."

The merchant handed the knife back and said, "Wait here."

He shuffled across the room between the piles of goods until he was out view. Onäm's short-tempered comment had attracted some of the crowd and men came up close behind us to watch the transaction. Then, after some time, the tradesman returned, carrying a sheath with a knife in it.

"This is the finest knife I have, better even than yours."

I looked at the object in his hand and made to take it from him to examine, but he snatched away.

"Let's see the colour of your silver first."

There were shouts of agreement from behind us, and I sensed that the atmosphere was getting very unfriendly. It was clear from our accents that we were Svear men.

Erik was not one to shy from an argument. He took the purse from his belt, opened it, and showed the merchant the contents. Men behind him strained to get a view of it.

"The price is three aurar."

He passed the knife to me. There was no doubt: it was my knife.

"Do you expect me to buy my own knife!?" I shouted. "It was stolen from me."

Onäm leant forward and grabbed the merchant by the throat.

"Who sold you this knife?" he demanded.

Gasping for breath, the choking man said, in a voice as loud as he could muster, "It was a girl, a pretty girl."

Onäm now turned on me and said, "You didn't say it was a girl who attacked you."

There was laughter among the throng behind us.

I was so embarrassed. I spluttered, "She didn't, she was holding me."

The laughter in the crowd increased.

My uncle had heard enough. He looked behind and realised that the crowd would side with the merchant if he refused to pay. We were hugely outnumbered.

"Erik, give me your purse."

Onäm counted out three aurar, passed the purse back, and slammed the coins down onto the window sill.

As we pushed our way back out through the crowd, we were barged against, cursed, and threatened with fists.

"Come on, let's get back the house and keep out of trouble until our ship sails on the morrow."

As we walked through the crowded streets, Onäm, who had recovered his composure, turned to me and grinned. "So, you had a girl last night, but it cost you a bloody head and three aurar."

I decided not to answer.

The next day, we boarded a trading vessel bound for Svealand. Unlike the *Dragon*, it was fat bellied and somewhat shorter. In the middle of the ship, just behind the mast, there was a deep opening surrounded by a low wooden structure. We heard the sound and smelt the stink of cows as we stood on the quayside.

"Climb on!" the man who was standing at the stern shouted to us.

We clambered aboard, carefully avoiding the dung on the gunnel. Three cows stood in the cargo hold, restrained by ropes. The seaman shouted, "Three pregnant cows for Svealand!"

"You had better get used to this stench, we are keeping company with the animals for some days," said Onäm.

"Could be weeks, if the wind is foul," shouted the man, who we realised must be the captain. "You pay me half your voyage cost now and half when we get there."

While Onäm went aft to deal with the transaction, the three of us looked around the ship. There were two thwarts on each side astern of the mast and two forward of it. Crew were busying about dealing with the lines before casting off.

Onäm returned and said, "We take two of the bow forward thwarts and two of the aft ones. You can choose."

I realised that the further forward I sat, the wetter I would get from spray if the weather got bad. However, to be sitting behind the mast I would be downwind of the stench of the cattle.

In the hope of good weather I said, "Erik and I will go forward."

"You put your trust in the weather gods!" commented Onäm, laughing.

"Where is the ship going?" I asked as the captain joined us.

"Further north than Aros. We will put you ashore in the nearest port," he said.

"Where do you go then?"

"Two days north of where we leave you, we go into a mighty river and up to a settlement where they produce the best iron. We trade the cows for iron."

"A good trade, we hear that you Geats have no iron," said Onäm.

"A very good trade, good iron is expensive here."

Shortly after, we cast off and started our voyage.

CHAPTER 12

Borresta, Svealand, the year 991

We heard the sound of the dogs barking long before we emerged from the pine forest-lined track that led to the village. The heavy morning dew remained on the grass between the cartwheel ruts as we travelled in single file. I rode with my mounted companions, Erik and Onäm. Trudging along behind us was Elfgar, my thrall.

Onäm had taken me by surprise when we landed from the ship.

"We can travel the shortest way to Borresta, I have no plan to go to Aros."

"But won't you offer your services to the chieftain?" I asked.

"No, let younger ones do it. I have no family but those in Borresta. I have enough wealth to buy a farm."

I was really taken aback and said, "You are a warrior, not a farmer."

"I am an aging warrior with no woman, time for me to settle down."

"But you fought like a bear in the battle."

"Yes, and now I will enjoy my reward."

"And never get to Valhalla?"

"I am sure that I have deserved my place."

I thought for a moment. It would be a great advantage to my plans to have Onäm living at Borresta.

"Then come with us, the snows will be upon us soon."

As we entered the village, there were scenes of activity with men and women scurrying about. Gradually it ceased and the people stood staring at us as we dismounted and led our horses to the centre of the open space. I immediately spotted my mother coming towards us, carrying a tub. It was then I realised that the village folk, warned by the barking of dogs, had thought that we were the tithe collectors.

"Ulf, Ulf, is it you?" she said, still grasping the heavy tub. She looked so much older; there were lines on her face that had not been there before, and her hair had turned grey.

I took the tub, placed it on the ground, and threw my arms around her.

Then I turned and pointed, saying, "And look, I have a surprise for you. Do you know this man?"

She looked up at Onäm, her face creasing as she squinted to see his features.

"Do you recognise me, Sigrid?" he asked.

She grabbed his wrists with her hands, looked up at him, and said, "Your mother and father missed you, so did your sisters. Where have you been?"

"Many places, Sigrid, many places. But now I am come home to be a farmer."

"You are welcome; this is your village. We need more men."

"Where is my brother?" he asked.

"Yes, where is Father?" I added.

"Hafnir is dead."

I had seen many deaths since my departure from the village, but this was one that really shocked me.

"When? How?" I spluttered.

She sobbed as she answered, "Two winters ago, he was hunting. He never came home, but in the spring, what the wolves had left of his body was found near to the big farm. Some say that the wolves killed him, for they were very hungry that winter. Others say that in his hunt he strayed too close to the big farm, Birger's land, and the henchmen killed him."

My reflection on this bad news was interrupted by shouting nearby. I turned and saw a woman, whom I recognised to be Erik's mother, with a broom in her hands.

"You lazy wastrel. Where have you been?" she said as she brought the broom down on Erik's shoulder.

"But, Mother, but I couldn't...."

His pleading was cut off by another blow.

"Your father, good for nothing that he is, has had need of help. We are both getting old. And so where is our son? Where have you been?"

Erik grabbed the broom and looked across to Onäm and me as he tried to keep it out of her reach. We both burst out laughing.

"Tell her, will you, Ulf," pleaded Erik.

"It is true mistress; we couldn't return until now."

The woman started to calm down. She grabbed the broom from him, took a step backwards, and looked Erik up and down.

"True or not, now you can make up for the time you have been away. You have eaten well I can see, don't expect to do so here."

During this episode, Elfgar had gathered up the reins of the horses and loosened their girths. He had spotted the watering trough and led the animals over for a drink.

"Who is your friend?" asked my mother.

"That is Elfgar, he is my thrall."

"You have a horse and a thrall?"

"And more. But we are hungry, open the tub, let's try the chieftain's fish."

"But what if Ingemund should come to collect them?"

"Is he still collecting the tithes? Don't worry, we can buy more. Erik, come and join us."

Later, as we sat around the hearth in the room, which was once just adequate for my parents and me, I sat squeezed up on the bench with my companions and Elfgar, supping on the fish and Mother's bread. The Saxon was beginning to learn some Norse words, but he could not yet understand our conversation. I pulled up the stool from the weaving loom, indicated to Elfgar to leave us, and made a space for Mother.

"Come, Mother, sit and I will tell you of our plans."

She wiped her hands on her apron and joined us.

"We have much to tell you of our travels, the places we have seen, and the honour we have won, but first let me tell you that you will never go hungry again, for I have silver. We all have silver."

I took off my boot and showed her the heavy silver ring around my ankle.

"And I have more in the other boot."

"How did you get it?" she asked in astonishment.

"Never mind, I will tell you our story later."

"What are you going to do with it?"

"We are going to clear forest and build a farm. The three of us together, Onäm, Erik, and me."

"Will you leave me here alone?"

"No, of course not. Each of us will have a house and a share in the estate."

"When will you do this?"

"We will start tomorrow. Several of the villagers have land down by the lake, we'll offer them a good price for the right to use it."

The next day we started approaching villagers and began bargaining. At first, they were reluctant, but soon several agreed to our offers, especially when we told them that they could work for us to clear the forest and create new meadows. Eventually, some of our neighbours started to approach us, for they realised that as well as employing them we would also protect them. This realisation came about after our encounter with the tithe collectors just two days after we returned to Borresta.

"The dogs do bark, Ulf, it could be Ingemund. We have not replaced the fish in the tub."

"Don't worry, Mother, I'll deal with him."

Sure enough, a few minutes later the procession of four horses appeared from out of the pines, followed by a horse drawing a laden cart. The leading rider was instantly recognisable. Ingemund's face was thinner than ever, and his sparse grey beard had become even more scant, but there was no mistaking him.

The villagers scurried around to get their tithes ready to hand over.

"Well, look who is here, so the Geats didn't kill you, Ulf?"

"You heard what happened?"

"Yes, two of Gnir's men returned to tell the tale."

"They were lucky to get away."

"We have a new chieftain now, Ragnar. He's one of Thorkell's men, Earl Thorkell of the Jomsviking."

I had heard of the Jomsviking from Dragon's crew. They were legendary warriors who held sway to the south of the land of the Geats.

"And it is this Ragnar you now serve?"

"Yes, and he expects the tithes to be paid as before." Turning to his men, he called, "Come on, get to work."

They dismounted and started to open the tubs of fish.

"Where's your fish?" demanded Ingemund of me.

"I have only just returned; I have had no time to fish."

Ingemund glowered at me and then shouted to one of the warriors, "Go, that house over there, take whatever you can find."

The man strode towards the door of our house, but as he did so, the door opened and Onäm came out. He had his sword belt on.

"Stand aside, peasant," said the warrior to Onäm.

"And if I don't?"

"I'll have your head on a pole, a warning to others."

They glared at each other as both men drew their swords and moved away from the front door. Then Elfgar appeared from the house, carrying my sword.

As the other two warriors started to run towards Onäm to help their comrade, Erik followed not far behind. At that moment I saw that Ingemund was drawing his sword. I was unarmed. I had to stop him. Then I remembered the spear he kept under his saddle. I grabbed it and slid it forward. He was no warrior, for as soon as he saw that the tip was pointed at him, he pushed his sword back into the scabbard. While he was doing this, there was a loud curse from one of his men as Erik pounced on his back and forced him to the ground.

Onäm's sword was clanging against his opponent's, but not for long. He made one of his characteristic leaps and the confused warrior was floored by the impact of Onäm's sword on his helmet. Meanwhile, Elfgar was standing, with a broad grin on his face, pointing my sword at the only man not on the ground.

The threat was sufficient; Ingemund's man lowered his sword and offered no resistance.

"Ingemund, how much are the tithes from Borresta worth to Ragnar?" I shouted.

"Um … perhaps three auras of silver."

I had no coin left after the robbery, only the silver bands we had detached from my ankles.

"Erik, come here," I called. "Open your purse, give him three coins."

He fumbled with his money belt and identified three of the Ethelred silver coins. He handed them to me.

"Then take this to Ragnar. Greet him from Ulf, Onäm, and Erik of Borresta, warriors who have fought with the great Olaf Tryggvason in Aenglandi. Tell him that the people of Borresta wish to keep their food for the winter."

"I will," bleated Ingemund, and then he added hesitatingly, "What about my men?"

"Take them and have them act more kindly next year."

After the procession had gone, Erik said, "You use my money freely, Ulf. We must have a reckoning."

"It's true, we must. For you have paid three aurar for my knife and now my share of payment to the chieftain, one aura."

"And I paid for the ship's passage," said Onäm.

"Come, let's settle these affairs over an ale," I suggested.

We settled our affairs amicably, aware that I had less silver than the others because I had bought Elfgard. In the end we agreed that he would help with our work and, through the value of this, we would say that all three of us had an equal share in the venture ahead of us.

CHAPTER 13

In the first weeks back in Borresta, we also bought the rights to small areas of forest, and gradually our landholding increased. This was made easier because of the honour we three warriors had gained by our treatment of Ingemund and his men. The work was hard. In the spring following our return, the forest echoed to the thud of axes and the crash of pine trees falling to the ground. Most difficult was removing the roots of the trees we had felled and later clearing boulders to make open fields.

We never heard any complaint from the chieftain, Ragnar; he was no doubt pleased to get a silver payment. And the following year, because we had bigger fields to farm and those who worked for us fished together instead of every man competing with the next, the tithes were paid in the old way, leaving more than sufficient for the needs of the village.

It was when we were building the first house on the farm that my mother came with our morning food one day in the company of another woman of about her age, whom I recognised as Helga, wife of Crooked Nose Arne. Trailing shyly behind them was a young woman. I knew her well - I used to play with Astrid before I was of an age when boys don't play with girls.

The women busied themselves about preparing our food. When we stopped to eat, Mother said, "See how handy Astrid is now that she is a woman."

Erik turned to me and, clumsy as he usually was, not realising that he might be heard, said, "She is well ready to be bedded, Ulf."

"You watch your tongue, Erik. Don't embarrass the poor girl," said Mother.

She then proceeded to do just that.

"Young Astrid will marry in good time, but it will be to a real man, not an ale swilling sot like you."

It was true. Erik had quickly gained a reputation for his weakness for the strong ale, and I feared that his silver would not last long. This worried me because of our agreement about equal shared ownership of our enterprise.

Erik was suitably chastened by Mother's remark and we got on with our eating. As Astrid served the small beer she leant forward, and her breast brushed against my shoulder. I began to feel a fire in my loins that was not quenched as I began to observe her working. Thankfully, she had not inherited her father's nose. During the years we had been away, she had become quite comely. Her name meant "divine beauty," and while that was an exaggeration in her case, she was a well-shaped girl.

Later, Mother whispered to me, "I noticed you watching Astrid. You need a wife to keep this house for you when it is finished. You could do worse than taking her."

"Her father has the forest next to the big farm, Birger's land, doesn't he?"

"Yes, why?"

"Onäm made Crooked Nose an offer, but he refused to sell."

"The old man is a stubborn fool, but he works hard."

"Tell Helga that I am interested in getting to know her girl, but only if the old man relents and considers our offer."

And so it was I took a wife and increased our lands further. Astrid was a good woman; she was kind and obedient, though when I lay between her legs I always imagined I was with Hana. The image of the dark-haired girl still haunted me.

It was a good thing to have taken her as a wife, for in quick succession she gave me two sons, Dag and Halvar. It was the third time she was with child, four years later, that the gods favoured us no longer. Astrid died a slow death with child-birth fever. Her mother blamed me and perhaps others did too, saying that I had not been generous enough in my sacrifices to the gods. When she had gone, I tried to bring up the boys myself, but I was always very busy managing our affairs. I had little time for them. My mother and Elfgar tried to keep them from being too wild and disobedient.

By this time, our harvests gave enough corn for the needs of the village and some over to sell. I travelled to Aros each autumn with a cart full of grain to sell in the market, though it was a long and hazardous journey. That is where I bought two women slaves, a Rus and a Frisian. Together with Elfgar, they ran the household under the strict eye of my mother. The girl from the east lands was called Stanislava, though we called her Slava. She caught Elfgar's eye soon after she arrived, and I was happy for them to enjoy each other. The Frisian woman, Femke, brought me some solace and warmed my bed from time to time.

The transaction with Crooked Nose was the worst part of the marriage bargain, for the land we bought from him brought us often into conflict with Birger and his henchmen. Though there were arguments about where the boundary was between us, and occasionally our workers came to blows, we never came into armed hostility. Birger was too clever for that, for he knew that apart from the three warriors of Borresta, Onäm had trained

Elfgar and some of the strongest men in the village to handle arms. So, we lived in an uneasy peace with our neighbour.

Erik chose a local girl, Inger, to marry, and she gave him a son and a daughter. As time went on, he became less enthusiastic about our farming enterprise and his unreliability became a worry. Several times I reminded him of the poverty and hunger that we had experienced as children and how good things were now. But generally, we lived in harmony. Apart from news I brought back from Aros, we knew little of what was happening in the world beyond our borders, and traveller's tales were always exciting to us. It was a shock to us when Ingemund told us the news that Olaf Tryggvason was killed in a sea battle near the island of Svold, defeated by Jarl Thorkell, who men called Thorkell the Tall, the chieftain of the Jomsviking.

Occasionally, Onäm, Erik, and I sat sharing ale, relishing retelling the stories of those we had fought together with and wondering which of them were still going a-viking. At times like this, the three of us all felt the urge to set sail again. But once the effect of the drink had worn off, we realised that we had a good life here and no need of such adventures. But one unwanted adventure did come our way just after the feast of Lithasblot, a month after the longest day.

"Elfgar, go and see why the dogs are barking," I ordered as Slava, Femke, Onäm, Elfgar, the two boys, and I sat eating evening food.

He soon returned. "There are three men standing by the gate."

We had a wooden fence of sharpened upright poles all around the animal pens, the barn, and the three houses to protect the livestock from wolves and keep out any unwanted visitors, always conscious that Birger might be foolish enough to cause trouble. Because of this the villagers called the farm Ribbagård – "farm with poles."

"Who are they?"

"Priests, from my religion, shaven heads. They're on foot. They have no horses."

"What can they be doing here?" I asked. I was disappointed, for I had hoped that they might be interesting travellers with stories to tell us.

"Probably trying to convert us to their ways. Keep them away from me," said Onäm.

"Me too. They can sleep in the barn if they want shelter," I said to Elfgar.

I looked through the wooden shutter as he went out to speak to them. They were all wearing unseasonably long black cloaks. Two of them were shaven heads, the other had a large cowl that also covered most of his face, even though the evening was warm. Elfgar was directing them to the barn. At that time of year, the animals were all out in the open, so if the shaven heads used some clean straw, they would have a good night's sleep.

"Femke, prepare some porridge for our visitors."

When the food was ready, I ordered her to take it to the barn.

"Dag, you go with Femke."

Dag was now a boy of eleven summers. He was a sturdy lad, and though quite wilful, he was beginning to be very handy around the farm.

After some time, I commented, "Where are they, they have taken a long time, it will be getting dark soon."

"Beware, Ulf, perhaps they are converting Femke and Dag to the new religion," joked Onäm.

Just then there was a woman's scream. The door burst open and Femke, very short of breath, gabbled, "They have swords, they have taken Dag."

"The shaven heads are armed?" stuttered Elfgar.

Femke started sobbing violently, "Yes, yes, they tried to take me too, but Dag kept them busy, he tried to fight them."

"Is he all right? What have they done to him?"

"I don't know, I ran away. Please, please go to help him!"

Onäm dashed out of the house, shouting back to me that he was going to get his sword.

"Meet me back here, there must be some reason for this attack. We must be careful."

I armed myself and gave Elfgar a spear, and he pulled out his seax, the long knife the Saxons liked to carry, from his wooden chest.

"You women folk, stay in the house, you too, Halvar," I commanded as Elfgar and I went out to meet Onäm.

The sight we were greeted with was an appalling one. The so-called priests had thrown off their cloaks and stood in a line. The man in the centre, whose head was not shaven, was holding Dag with his right arm tightly around the boy's neck.

"You have done well, Ulf, from a slave boy to a rich farmer," called the man in the middle.

I first recognised the voice and then the face. The livid scar I had caused was still there.

In disbelief, I stammered, "Agmunder, but ... but you were killed."

"And no thanks to you, I would have died if the Geat village folk hadn't kept me alive to serve as a slave."

"Let the boy go and you shall have the satisfaction you once craved, to face me with the sword."

"Oh no, I'm sure one of your henchmen would kill me anyway, with an arrow or a spear."

"No, just you and me."

"You heard my answer. I heard that you won Danegeld in Aenglandi. I want a share. My share. I should have been with you there if you had not plotted against me."

"The silver is long gone, spent on our farm."

"I don't believe you." He pulled out his knife with his left hand and, keeping his arm round Dag's neck, passed the knife to his right hand. He then pulled Dag's ear out with his free hand and put the knife to it.

Then a figure appeared round the corner of the barn. It was Erik. He was waddling along some way behind the three men. His house was beyond the barn, and he had not been observed by the three intruders. In his hand was his bow, but he was obviously very drunk.

I had to keep the attention of the men in the hope that despite his condition, Erik might be able to shoot Agmunder in the back. I had to keep them talking.

"How did you get back to Svealand, Agmunder?"

"I killed my Geat master and stole his horse."

Erik was swaying to and fro as he raised his bow. At any moment one of the men might look behind them. I willed him to let an arrow fly.

"Have you become Christianised?" I said, pointing at the supposed priests.

The laughter of the three men was punctuated by the whoosh of an arrow and the scream of one of the shaven headed men. As the man fell, Agmunder turned to see where the arrow came from, and as he did so, he deliberately sliced off Dag's ear.

Addressing Erik and holding the bloody ear aloft he shouted over the screams of Dag, "Here's the first ear, put down your bow or I will take next."

As Erik rocked back and forth, slowly taking in the import of the message, I saw a quick movement to my right. Elfgar had seen that momentarily, while Agmunder was turned towards Erik, Dag was sheltered by the big man's body.

Elfgar's spear struck Agmunder between the shoulder blades. Onäm's training had not been wasted on the Saxon.

Agmunder moaned loudly as the weapon embedded in his back caused him first to release Dag and then to stagger forward, before falling at Erik's feet.

The third assailant made to grab Dag as the boy very shakily tried to run towards me, blood flowing down his shoulder. Onäm leapt forward, and his sword came down heavily in a diagonal cut into the man's neck.

I rushed towards the boy and threw my arms around him. Then I pulled his hair back to look at the wound. It was ghastly. The blood was pumping down his neck and chin. I drew him towards me trying to console his shock and pain as the red fluid stained my tunic. My rage had taken over. I was beside myself with fury. I passed the boy to Femke as she arrived at the scene of the carnage and I turned to Erik.

"You drunken fool, you hit the wrong man. Because of you Dag is wounded!" I shouted.

He swayed from side to side as he said, "If it hadn't … if it hadn't been for me, he might have been killed, you ungrateful bastard."

Onäm put his arm round my shoulder and said, "Calm down, Erik is right. It could have been worse for us."

I pushed him away and stood in silence, glowering at Erik, then turned on my heel and marched to the house to see how the boy was, leaving the others to plunder the bodies and dispose of them.

CHAPTER 14

Dag bled terribly for some days and then got a fever. We feared for his life, but the village wise woman used potions and spells which, after some days, were effective. Within a few weeks, he was completely healed, but nothing we could do would stop the village boys calling him "Dag One Ear." What I had told Agmunder was true, most of our Danegeld silver was long gone, although the money I made from selling grain allowed us to supplement our wealth. We also did some affairs with travelling fur traders and were paid in silver.

The knowledge that our village was no longer poor had spread widely and from time to time travelling vendors visited us to sell their wares. It was hardly surprising when Erik declared that he had no silver left, for whenever a trader visited us, he always bought some item, a trinket for Inger, his wife; a flask of mead; or some other unnecessary luxury. Then, two summers after the incident with Agmunder, Erik started to "disappear" for many hours at a time. The fact that he was missing when we were doing tasks that required his help eventually caused much friction between us. Finally, my patience was exhausted.

"Where in the gods' names have you been!?" I demanded.

"It's none of your concern. I do as I want."

His speech was slurred, and I could smell the beer on his breath.

"You can take all the ale you wish in the evenings, but in the daytime, we need your help. We have more tall pines to fell before the days get cold, to build our water mill."

"Well soon you will not have my help, for I am going to be rich again."

"What in the name of Odin do you mean?"

"Birger wishes to buy my share in the farm, and he will pay me a good price in silver."

"You drunken sot, is it to Birger's farm you go to get your ale?"

Erik paused, suddenly aware that while he was the bigger of the two us, I was sober and fired with rage. He saw too that I was carrying a hand axe.

"You fool, Erik, Birger is our rival, his men constantly cause problems for us. I will kill you before letting you sell your share."

I raised the axe, but then slowly let it fall, avoiding Erik.

"But Birger's a wealthy man, he can help you to get more land."

"Never, the man is a scoundrel."

Onäm had heard the raised voices and appeared carrying a pile of fire logs, followed by his elk hound.

"What's wrong, Ulf?"

"This lazy, drunken cur has been spending time with Birger," I spat out with disdain.

"So, that is where you have been spending your time."

"But the worst thing is, he wants to sell his share of the farm to Birger."

"I will carve the guts out of him if he tries," threatened Onäm.

Erik, sensing the danger he was in, stepped back.

"I've had enough of farming, I want to become a warrior again," said Erik pathetically.

"We'll buy your damned share, just give us time to get silver," I said.

"That'll take years," bleated Erik.

"Perhaps, but if you propose selling to Birger again, you won't live to see any silver."

I raised the axe again to reinforce my threat and then turned to leave. I turned back and said, "Tomorrow at first light we go to fell the tall pines, you too, Erik."

Our confrontation had been overheard by others and the word quickly spread that all was not well at the farm. Eventually, through travelling traders, the news must have reached the chieftain, Ragnar. We discovered this at the time of the first frosts when, the next year, Old Ingemund the tithe collector, now looking more pinch faced and wrinkled than ever, had a message for me.

"It has come to the attention of Ragnar, our chieftain, that you are in want of silver here at Ribbagård." His once strident tone was now gone, and his voice was tremulous and more difficult to hear.

I was irritated.

"Are our affairs here so public that they have become gossip in Aros?" I demanded.

"Well, you know where the blame for that lies," he said, beckoning towards Erik.

Erik looked unabashed. His performance in sharing the work of the farm reflected his declining commitment.

"I bear a message from Ragnar."

I went forward to stand by his horse so that we might speak privately.

"Ragnar owes allegiance to Thorkell the Tall, the man who defeated Olaf Trygvasson, your previous leader. Thorkell is a great warrior. He has called the Aros housecarls to join his army to raid Aenglandi after the snow melt next year."

I felt a thrill at the mere mention of the country. Ingemund recognised my interest and warmed to his subject.

"Thorkell will gain great wealth for his men, and they will have the honour of serving with him."

"When will they travel from Aros?"

"As soon as the ice breaks, vessels will be launched and leave for the meeting place in the land of the Geats at their fortress."

"Ragnar knows of the valour of you and your two companions, that you were among the great warriors who fought with Tryggvason at Maeldun."

"But our deeds in Aenglandi were many years ago, almost twenty summers since."

"Nevertheless, he wants you and two others to join the housecarls. As a village chief, you know you have a duty to do so if it is required."

While Ingemund was about his business collecting the goods from the villagers, I took Onäm aside and gave him the news.

"I am an old man now, Ulf, perhaps of about fifty-five summers, I cannot fight as once I did."

"But, Onäm, this is a chance for us to earn another Danegeld and buy Erik's share of Ribbagård."

"At my age, it is a good chance to be killed."

"We have a duty to supply three men to join Thorkell," I pointed out.

"Then take Erik. He is longing to blood his spear again."

"He needs an occupation to keep him from the company of Birger."

"If you can keep him from the ale, he will be good company."

"But we must be three."

"You have an elder son who gets bigger and stronger by the day."

"Dag?"

"He is of seventeen summers is he not?"

"But he is a boy," I said.

"More of a man than you were when you were taken to Aros with Erik."

"True, we were younger."

"Through the winter, I will train him to use arms."

I thought for a moment and then slapped Onäm on the shoulder and quipped, "That way I might get two shares of the Danegeld."

"Elfgar and I will look after the farm while you are away. He has a sword now, he took one from one of the dead shaven heads. Dag can take the other one."

Before Ingemund left, I told him to give Ragnar the message that there would be three armed men joining the housecarls when the winter thaw came.

CHAPTER 15

Sandwich, southern England, the year 1009

In the fog it had been difficult to form all the ships into a line abreast. We had been ordered to keep absolutely quiet, so commands were whispered. Even the sound of creaking carried long distances in the wet mist. The commander, Thorkell, required us to advance to the shore together in a parallel line so that we might overwhelm the town by surprise. We had been told that Sandwich was the most important port in the whole of Angleandi. We had high hopes to benefit from the wealth of the town.

The fleet was as big as ever could have been seen. We had sailed from the land of the Danes with the jarl and met up with two other fleets off the island they call Thanet. The other fleets were commanded by Eiglaf and Hemming, Thorkell's brother. It was said that there were a hundred ships, and most of them carried at least fifty men.

In the fog we could see one ship on either side of us, but only the dark shapes of the ones next to them. It was soon clear that the power of the tide was making it impossible to remain in line. Every captain wanted to be the first to the shore, and each crew knew that those who came last would have least plunder.

We watched the neighbouring ships to see who broke the line first, and of course, as far as they could, they were watching us.

"The damned current pushes us sideways," commented Erik as he sat impatiently watching the next ship, the handle of his oar already dipped and the blade raised in readiness for the order.

"The sooner we get there the better," said Dag. "Today I will blood my sword."

Dag's enthusiasm to see action for the first time worried me. He had become friends with some other young warriors, real hotheads, and fallen under their influence. All of them were inexperienced but eager to fight. I feared that Dag's wilfulness, combined with his anxiety to impress, would lead him to be reckless in battle.

"Stay with me after we have landed," I instructed him.

He did not answer.

"Together!" called the captain quietly. Those who sat nearer the bow did not hear the order, but all saw what those in front of them were doing.

"Pull!" he shouted loudly. His order was echoed by others, mostly unseen, on both sides of us.

The attack had begun.

There was a crunch as our ship grounded on a sandy shore covered with patches of small stones. We leapt over the side into the shallow sea, and together the crew pulled the ship as far as we could up the beach. In front of us there was no sign of life, and in the fog we could see only a long ridge of rounded pebbles. When the crews had all assembled, we armed and started trudging over the ridge, Dag and his friends leading our crew. The stones made walking difficult and running impossible. There was a loud roar of crunching as hundreds of men traversed the ridge. Beyond it we found flat land with tufted sea grass and proceeded more quickly as the fog began to lift.

"It's no good, Ulf, you'll never keep up with him," panted Erik.

"The boy's mind is so full of visions of gaining honour and plunder that he acts as foolishly as the other wild ones," I answered.

The gap between the vanguard and we older men suddenly started to shorten.

"That stopped them, they are getting a taste of Saxon arrows," said Erik.

The noise of the rattling stones had clearly alarmed the Saxons, and several bowmen were firing at the advancing Norsemen. A number of our bowmen hurried forward and returned the fire. Soon we advanced again, and as we did so we passed several dead, dying, and wounded warriors.

"The Saxons will pay dearly for this," I said.

What happened next was to repeat itself many, many times as we roamed and ravaged all over the south of the country. We took from the Saxons what we wanted and killed many of them. After taking Sandwich we took Canterbury, and there the people of the town sued for peace, paying us three thousand pounds of silver. There was no thought of taking slaves, for we did not want extra mouths to feed as we plundered and burnt our way through the land. Occasionally, we met with Saxon levies, mostly untrained farmers. After short battles, they always fled the field. Earl Thorkell was well satisfied with our booty but he had increasing difficulty in keeping discipline among his men. He was used to commanding the Jomsviking, where those who disobeyed would be put to the sword, but in this great army, among the true warriors, there were many savage scoundrels. Bestial men whose cruelty against defenceless women and children sometimes shamed us. Increasingly, Thorkell tried to stop the burning and mindless violence, reasoning that if the towns and villages were destroyed, they could not be plundered again in the future. For the same reason, he tried to limit the killing so that the Saxons could rebuild their homes. But his voice became more and more unheard in the bloody mayhem.

As winter approached, and as it was too late in the season for us to sail home, the commander decided that we should overwinter in the country. There was a rumour that the king in the great city by the river Thames was gathering a large army against us. The winter was not a good time to fight, so we moved from place to place to avoid a battle. In the spring, we boarded our ships and sailed north to the land of the East Saxons.

As our ship followed the convoy in front of us into the harbour, I felt a thrill.

"I know this place; don't you recognise it, Erik?"

"This is where we found the mill, what was the place called?"

I was almost breathless with excitement.

"Gippeswic. Do you think that my woman is still here?"

"If she is, she'll have had a husband for many years."

"Yes, I should remember, it is almost twenty years since we were here. Even if Hana still lives, she will be almost an old woman now."

"You are older too," commented Erik.

"What will you do if you find her?" asked Dag. He had been listening to our conversation.

"I will take her home to Borresta, for I have no woman and the farm needs one."

"Let's go to the mill as soon as we land," said Erik.

170

"We'll have to hurry before the wild ones among the crews burn it."

Once more, there was no room for our ship in the harbour, and as dusk fell, we ran the bow through the reeds and grounded in the mud. The ill-disciplined crews had already started to plunder the town and set light to buildings. Erik, Dag, and I used the reeds to wipe the mud from our boots, by the light of the flames. Ignoring the prospect of plunder in the town, we slipped through the huts and hovels and made our way in the darkness to the mill. We were not alone, for there was a stream of fleeing Saxon women and children, desperately making their way to a place of safety inland.

As we approached the building, Erik called, "Look, there is someone holding a lantern outside the building. Come on."

"Keep your sword in the scabbard, Dag, no killing here," I demanded as loudly as I dared without betraying our presence.

When we approached the mill, we could make out the shape of horses or donkeys milling around on the yard outside. We heard a slap, such as a beast's rump being hit to make it move. Then a clicking sound as someone urged an animal to hurry. We were within twenty paces when we saw the last of the animals disappearing into the darkness. All that was left was the bearer of the lantern. It was a man.

Our young warrior companion was, as usual, ahead of us.

"Grab him, Dag, don't kill him."

There was a short struggle and a thud as the lantern crashed onto Dag's head. Curiously, the light continued to burn as the lantern lay on its side on the ground.

"Hold the Saxon, Erik," I said distractedly, my attention being attracted to Dag, who, now on one knee, was pulling out his knife.

"No, Dag, no killing!" I shouted as I struggled to hold his right wrist. The boy's temper was aroused by the ignominy of being floored by a Saxon. I held him tightly for a while and then watched as he slowly replaced his knife.

The Saxon was pinioned against the door of the house by the weight of Erik. But the man was not ready to give in and kept attempting to kick the shins of his captor. Erik's patience was quickly exhausted, and he drew his knife and held it at the man's throat. I picked up the lantern.

"Let's look inside, open the door, Dag. Bring him in, Erik."

The inside of the house was just as I remembered it, but this time there was no sound of a woman screaming. I looked into the room where I had once sat with Hana and where Tor had met his end. I found myself doing something I realised was a habit whenever I had thoughts of Hana: I felt for the raised scar on my neck and gently stroked it.

I turned and asked, "Who are you?" and pointed quizzically at the Saxon. I had learned some of the language of the country during the year we had spent there, but he understood the Norse when I spoke very slowly.

"I am Oswald, but because of your foul kind, some call me Oswald the bastard."

"You fight well, Oswald. But I fear that you won't have a chance against the others who will soon join us."

"Why do they call you 'the bastard'?" asked Dag.

"For my mother was left pregnant by one of you heathen scum."

His petulance annoyed me, but I tried not to react. I held up the lantern to look at him more closely. He was a young man, not much older than Dag. He wore a grey tunic and round his shoulders was a green woollen cloak with a bright red pattern.

Unusually for a Saxon, his hair was dark, though not completely black. His dark eyes flashed with hatred.

My hand on the lantern trembled, and I gulped as I asked, "What is your mother's name?"

"What is it to you, pagan?"

I saw that he winced as Erik's grip on his arm, which was forced up his back, hardened.

I took out my knife and held it at his throat.

"Her name," I demanded.

He whispered quietly, "Hana."

"Then you are ... you are his...."

"Shut up, Erik."

"How long have you lived here?"

"All my life, I was born here. My mother's master never returned, and she took over the mill and bought her freedom."

Dag could contain himself no longer. "You mean that his mother was taken by you?"

"I believe so," I answered lamely as I sought to order my thoughts.

"Then he is my half-brother, is he not?"

We had been speaking quickly and it was obvious that the Saxon had not understood what was said. My previous anger at his insolence dissolved into admiration. He had considerable courage to insult three armed captors. I addressed him again, speaking slowly.

"How old are you, Oswald?"

"I don't know, perhaps eighteen, nineteen, or twenty summers."

I could contain myself no longer, "Did your mother take a man as a husband?"

"No, it is said that she received many offers, but she refused them all. That is the right of a Saxon woman."

"Where is your mother?"

"She rode off to safety as you came, together with the old slave woman, Wilfrun."

I was staggered, my heart pumping as if I were in combat. I had just missed her.

I paused, thinking what to do. "We'd never be able to find them in the dark, even if we run," I lamented.

There was a long silence and then I said to Oswald, "Why did you not go with them?"

"For I am to join the levy of Ulfcytel the Bold at Ringmere. There we will defeat you heathens."

"Who is the Ulfcytel?" I asked.

"A great leader in battle. Only six years ago, he caused the Dane Swein Forkbeard to flee the field in dishonour. He…"

Oswald was interrupted as the door burst open and two Viking warriors ran into the room brandishing swords. They saw that we had a prisoner.

"Leave the Saxon to us," shouted one.

"I'll spill his guts on the floor," snarled the other.

I unsheathed my sword and pointed it at the leading man.

"He's our prisoner," I shouted.

"We don't take prisoners, you know that."

Dag was now behind the two men, both of whom were menacing Erik and me. They had not noticed him in the poor light. I beckoned to him to take one of them. He did not move but stayed in the shadows. I tried once more to get him to help, but he remained motionless. Then it suddenly occurred to me why. Oswald was my oldest son; he would inherit the farm and leave Dag with nothing. The boy had obviously realised this and was happy to see Oswald killed.

My rage took me; I would stop at nothing to protect Hana's boy. Onäm had taught me how to take an opponent by surprise by striking from an unexpected direction. I slashed from the left with all my might.

The man in front of me crumpled and fell backwards, his neck almost severed through. In the lantern light, I saw Erik try to plunge his sword in the other warrior. He was too quick and side stepped.

"We can't let him go, it will be the worse for us if he tells others what has happened," I shouted.

Dag came out of the shadows with his seax in hand. As the Norseman faced Erik and me, sword in hand, swearing and cursing at us, Dag stepped forward and drew his knife across the man's throat from behind. He dropped his sword and clutched at his throat before tumbling on the floor.

I unbuckled the sword belt of the dying man.

"Here, take these and run as fast as you can," I said to Oswald.

I passed the Norseman's belt and his sword to Oswald. The Saxon was completely confused but saw his chance to escape and took it.

I blew out the lantern and said, "Quickly, out of here before others arrive."

CHAPTER 16

Ringmere, May 1010

It was in late spring, after we had taken the town of Gippeswic and the surrounding villages, that we marched north to meet the Saxons on a wide heath by the side of a lake called Ringmere. We attacked Ulfcytel's battle line with great confidence, for we had such belief in the leaders of our great army. Very soon after the fight was joined, one of the Saxon commanders, Thurcytel, who the warriors called, "Mare's Head," fled the field with his levies, leaving Ulfcytel and the men of the shire of Cambridge to face us. They were great warriors indeed and resisted us ferociously. They put the battle in the balance.

"Turn the flank, turn the flank," Earl Hemming, Thorkell's brother, ordered our crew.

We slashed and thrusted at the Saxons on the end of the battle formation in an attempt to attack them from the side of their line.

"Dag, wait. Wait for more to join us before going further, we need more men," I called desperately as the rest of the crew fought their way to join us.

"You may wait, I will not."

His young companions laughed and jibed at Erik and me as we cajoled the crew to hurry, for we were well outnumbered.

"Come on, old man, or are you afraid?"

"Yes, show us how you fought at Maeldun, or have you forgotten?"

Erik was enraged, and for a moment I thought he might throw his spear at one of the young bloods.

"Look out, the Saxon flank is turning towards you!" I shouted.

It was just then that I recognised a man; it was the green and red cloak that caught my attention. Oswald had no helmet or shield and was in a line of men facing Dag and his comrades. Dag recognised him too and rushed in his direction, sword held high.

"No, no, Dag!" I yelled at the top of my voice, trying to overcome the shouting, swearing, screaming of wounded and crashing of swords on to shields, to make myself heard. Then I lost sight of the half-brothers.

"Come, Erik, hurry," I said, abandoning my hesitation.

We ran into the turmoil of the clash between our young warriors and the Saxon flank. As we did so, there was the sound of a horn being blown three times. It was clearly a signal from the Saxon commander for his men to re-group, for those on the flank started to withdraw. As they did so, I was horrified to see Dag struck down with a blow on the top of his helmet from Oswald. He fell to his knees. The Saxon lifted his sword to strike again but as he did so, he hesitated. He looked up and saw me. He lowered his sword slowly before turning and starting to run to join his withdrawing companions. One of Dag's friends lifted his spear, taking aim at Oswald's back. Erik was nearest. He leapt forward and struck the spear with his sword.

"You mad bastard, why did you do that?" screamed the furious young warrior as he raised his sword, threatening Erik.

"Don't threaten me, you snivelling whelp," answered an incensed Erik, levelling his own sword.

The younger man was too fast for Erik. Before I could intervene, the teenager landed a sword slash across Erik's shoulder.

He was joined by other young bloods. First one, then several of them attacked Erik, hacking him to the ground. Erik made not a sound. His helmet tumbled off, leaving him totally vulnerable to the retribution of the youths.

"Stop, stop, you fools! We have other business."

As I spoke, a group of Saxon horsemen thundered across the field towards our exposed group. The young warriors had never faced armed riders before. At first, they froze in horror, then started to run towards the main body of our army. Before running many paces, several succumbed to the spears of the horsemen.

I was left alone with the dead and the dying. I rushed over to where I had seen Dag fall. He was now on his back, but his eyes were open. I could only just see them as the blow from Oswald had forced his helmet hard down on his head. He was definitely breathing, and there were no obvious wounds to his body. I gently pulled his helmet off.

"How is it, Dag?"

"Is that you? Is that you, Father?"

"Yes, don't you see me?"

"I see nothing, just blackness."

As I tried to sit him up, he howled with pain.

"My head, it throbs and pulses. My neck and shoulders ache such as I have never known."

I regularly cast anxious glances up at the battle, it was still raging not more than fifty paces away. We were very exposed.

"Sit here a while, I must tend to Erik."

"Is he wounded?"

"Sorely, by your friends."

"But why?"

I chose not to answer and walked over to where Erik was writhing on the ground and quietly moaning. His stomach had been ripped open by a sword slash and his body pierced in several places. I had seen many men, mainly Saxons, with similar wounds during our rampage across the country. I knew that he would die, very slowly and in pain.

"Is the boy alive?" whispered Erik.

"I don't know which one you mean, but Dag is alive, and Oswald was when their army regrouped."

"Thank you, Ulf."

"For what?"

"For being my friend." He gulped, obviously suffering badly from the searing pain of his wounds.

"Thank you for saving my life many times, and now that of my son."

He was silent for a while, then said, "If you get Danegeld after this battle, take my share to Inger and take care of her."

"I will, Erik, I will."

"Now do one thing for me, Ulf, cut my throat."

"No, I will strike your heart. It will be quicker."

"Yes, you always were cleverer than me."

Erik nodded as he looked at the sword hovering above him. I hesitated, mesmerised by his display of incredible courage. He nodded again. I wished I could have closed my eyes, but I had to be sure that I hit him in a spot where death would be quick. With all the force I could muster, the weapon plunged deep into his chest.

To avoid the victors of the battle plundering his body, I emptied Erik's money belt, and from his wrist I slid off a silver bracelet he had taken from a dead Saxon in Canterbury. I would give it to his wife. I hid his sword under his body and then turned my attention to Dag. I stayed to protect him should the battle move our way again and watched as the fighting ranged to and fro. Eventually, the men of the shire gave way and Ulfcytel's standard was struck.

"There will be many grieving widows this night," called one of our men as he and a companion paused in passing.

"The slaughter has been immense on both sides," commented his companion.

"What of Jarl Thorkell?" I asked.

"He lives, but his brother, Hemming, is dead. As is Jarl Eiglaf."

"Many of the Saxon nobles are dead too. It is said that the son-in-law of their king and the grandson of Earl Byrhtnoth, our adversary at Maeldun, are dead as well," said the other.

I watched as they executed a wounded Saxon warrior who was lying nearby and then started to pull off the valuable chain mail shirt he had been wearing. Suddenly I was gripped with panic. I had to see if Oswald was among the wounded before the plunderers reached him. But I could not leave Dag. I pulled him to his feet and ignored his protests as I put one of his arms over my shoulder and started dragging him towards Earl Thorkell's standard, where it would be safe to leave him for a while.

I then hurried around the field of battle, among the scavengers and those who had still not satisfied their lust to kill, and searched frantically for any sign of the green and red cloak. In vain, I continued my search until darkness started to descend. "He must have escaped," I told myself. But I resolved to continue my search in the morning. My mind was in turmoil. My son was blind, my best friend was dead by my hand, and I knew not what fate had overtaken Oswald.

Wearily, I shouldered my shield and picked my way through the dead and the dying, back to where I had left Dag. He was sitting with his head in his hands, sobbing. I dragged him to his feet and, with the help of some of his friends, Erik's butchers, got him back to the ship. I was vengeful towards the young warriors but too tired, and perhaps too wise, to challenge them.

I spent the next morning searching the corpses; there was a multitude of them. In death some men looked blindly at the sky, many with faces contorted by the pain of the slaughter. Others hid their faces in the red mud. I was not alone. Some other Norsemen were plundering what was left of value; others were just searching for missing friends. But there were also women and children. Normally, women would hide from us and for good reason. Now in their desperation to find loved ones, they ignored the risk. Some cursed me as I passed them but I paid them no attention. Here and there, shaven heads supervised the lifting of bodies onto carts, probably the remains of high-ranking men. I picked my way past bodies lying in ghastly confusion, respectfully trying to avoid stepping on them. As I made my way through them, carrion crows squawked and flapped their wings, angry at being disturbed. Nowhere did I find a dead man with a green and red cloak.

By noon, I was convinced that Oswald had survived the battle. In the afternoon, I dug a trench next to where Erik's body lay and then rolled his corpse into it. As befits a warrior killed in battle, I placed his sword with him before filling the hole. I searched around to find some rocks and piled them on top of the grave. As is our way, I spent the night at the graveside. In the ceremony of "high sitting," after a period of fasting, I tried to find contact with Erik, and in grieving I hoped that the spirits of the dead might help me to decide what to do. It was eerily quiet apart from the sound of the crows that returned to the bodies at sunrise. There was no sound of jubilation or celebration from the victor's ships, a sure sign that the battle had been a very close-run affair and that many men were mourning lost friends. By dawn I had made up my mind. In the increasing light I started back to the ship to find Dag. There I found him, sitting on his thwart with his head in his hands.

"Dag, Thorkell's men have captured a great many horses, so now the army can raid far in land much more easily."

"But what is to become of me, for you know, already the crew taunt me because I have one ear and no eyes."

I knew I had to take the boy home but first I wanted my share of the spoils.

"We'll wait with the fleet until the king of this land agrees to pay a Danegeld. With this battle lost and our army raiding where they will on horseback, he must soon offer us riches in silver to leave his country."

And so we spent many months and even another winter with the men, many of them with wounds, who stayed on the ships to guard the fleet while the army was inland. We hungered for news of the campaign, and so when a group of men came back to the fleet, we were keen to hear their tidings.

"The jarl has made peace with the king!" announced a rough looking fellow with a fresh cut on his cheek and a ripped cloak.

"On what terms?" I asked.

"Thorkell has pledged allegiance to Ethelred. We are to get a Danegeld of five hundred thousand aurar of silver."

We were stunned by the size of the payment.

"Has the king so much silver?" I asked.

"And more," he said.

"You haven't told him everything," said his companion.

The man with the cut face added, "Oh yes, the jarl has pledged that our army will defend Ethelred from any further raids from the Norse. Not only that, but he has also promised to follow the new religion, the followers of the cross."

"And he has said that we all have to do so too," added the other man, laughing.

"What happened to you?" I asked, pointing at his cut.

"Rebels. Those Norsemen who defy the jarl, for many have paid no heed to the agreement with the king and continue to plunder and burn."

"We were in Canterbury, the rebelling Norse captured chieftains of the church and tried to ransom them. They had the most important priest in the land imprisoned. Thorkell offered them everything he had, except his ship, to let the priest go. But they refused and killed the holy man when he would not allow a Danegeld."

"Yes, when they saw we are Thorkell's men, they attacked us."

"We have enough men to crew a ship, so we are going to sail for home as soon as we get our share of the silver."

Over the next few weeks, many more warriors arrived and then a wagon load of silver to be shared between the men on the ships. There were fights and scuffles about the weighing of the shares but, eventually, we all had fifty aurar of silver each. With this done, the thoughts of many, including me, turned to voyaging home with our spoils. Many of the ships' captains decided to use the early autumn winds, which blew from Aenglandi towards the northlands, to return home before the winter storms. I found a passage for Dag and me.

As soon as we had finished rowing out of the river, we set sail. I gazed wistfully at the shore.

"Dag, you know my heart longs to stay here."

"Do you long for the woman or the boy?"

I hesitated, lifting my hand to feel the scar on my neck and then said, "Both."

"You would leave me without inheritance?"

"If necessary, but you would want for nothing."

"I want for two eyes, for I cannot manage the farm without them."

I hesitated again, deep in thought, watching the coast slipping away and with it my chance of fulfilling a dream. I answered, "No, you couldn't."

CHAPTER 17

Borresta, Svealand 1011

Even before we saw the village, the dogs started barking. It was nearly the dusk of an early winter day as we approached the gates of Ribbagård. They were already closed for the night.

"No great welcome for us, Dag, the gates are closed," I said as I pulled the horse on which he was riding towards me. I had been leading his horse behind me on our journey from the coast.

"The dogs have heard us," said Dag.

I peeped through a small spy hole in the door to see if there were others inside who had been alerted.

"Here comes Onäm," I reported to Dag.

"Have you room for two weary travellers?" I called through the hole.

"Ulf? Ulf, is that you?"

"The very same."

We heard Onäm shouting to others inside the stockade as he removed the bar locking the gates. Very soon we were inside and beset with questions.

"What has happened to you, Dag? Can you not see us?" asked Femke.

"He was sorely wounded in a savage battle at a place called Ringmere. He was outnumbered and took a sword blow to his head. It has left him blind. I hope he'll recover."

"Yes, it was a hard fight, but we put the Saxons to flight," said Dag.

"But where is his brother? Where is Halvar?" I asked.

The room went silent, and some of those in it anxiously glanced at each other. It fell to Onäm to speak.

"I have bad tidings, Ulf. Halvar went fishing last winter, before the ice had laid well. He has joined his great-grandfather with the water goddess."

"But how could you let him do that, Onäm?"

"I warned him many times, but he was a headstrong boy and paid little heed to what I said."

The atmosphere of our homecoming changed, especially when I learned that my mother had died while I was away. Dag was at first silent, grieving for his brother, but as the evening wore on, he contributed enthusiastically to my account of our voyage and the great battle. He was keen too to show everyone his share of the silver. Though he could not see them, he rejoiced in running the coins of Ethelred through his fingers and listening to the merry clink they made.

Elfgar, who had been very silent all evening, his loyalty to his own kind preventing him from taking enjoyment from our tale, asked, "But what of Erik? Is he on his way here too?"

It was my turn to break bad news, but I could not tell the truth. The fact that he had been felled by the wild hotheads who were Dag's friends was beyond telling.

"He died on the field of Ringmere. He was a great warrior who died heroically."

"We must tell his wife in the morning," said Elfgar.

186

"Yes, I must do it. I have some silver for her."

Later, much later, when the others had gone to their beds, I sat with Onäm. The ale had flowed freely; nevertheless, our mood was sombre. Gazing into the fire, his face illuminated by the dancing flames, Onäm said softly, "I am an old man, but I remember, I remember that things were never as simple in a battle as Dag made it sound this evening. Do you want to tell me what really happened?"

I waited a long time before answering, "There are some things best left untold, but I do not feel shame to say that I grieve for Erik as much as I do for Halvdar, my own dead son. Erik died because he saved someone else."

We were both silent for a while, and then he said, "Was it all worth it for the silver?"

"I am now a wealthy man. Yes, there has been a cost. I have lost my oldest and only true friend; my eldest son is blind and had I been at home, perhaps Halvdar would be alive.

There was another quiet time, both of us reflecting privately.

"Ulf, you can be proud, you have won great honour in two battles and gained Danegeld under Toste and then Thorkell. Now you have safely come home to live your life as a farmer, we should instruct the rune maker to record your story. A rune stone to stand outside the gate of Ribbagård."

As I stroked my scar, my feeling of profound unhappiness, lightened by a prospect beaming like a ray of sun through dark clouds, my vision was not of a rune stone, but of a woman and her son. It was a hope that I did not want to share with Onäm for fear of being ridiculed.

"Wait with the rune stone, Onäm, I am not finished."

"You will seek silver again?"

I was silent for a while as the flames flickered in front of me. I opened my clenched hands and ran them over my face. I let my eyes meet Onäm's. I said, "Yes, I must."

CHAPTER 18

After the turbulent life I had led for the last two years, it was difficult to resume the routine I had previously been used to at the farm. It was not made easier by the heavy burden of Erik's death. I tried to persuade myself that his death had averted a crisis in the ownership of our estate and his plan to sell to Birger. In any case, his love of ale would have increased with his age and caused strife within our small community. But it weighed heavily on my conscience that he had died at my hand. There too, I found myself tormented by thoughts about whether I could have done more to stop the hotheads attacking him. Even these thoughts were confused by the fact that he had given his life to save my son, a son who had previously caused Dag to be blind.

Dag suffered terribly from the indignity bestowed on him to need help with almost every task, but he was also in some pain with frequent aches of the head. These made him bad tempered and poor company. I found myself shunning spending time with him. I was glad that Elfgard attended to him. Thoughts of the future ownership of the estate concerned me too. Inger had inherited Erik's share, Onäm had no children, and I had a son who could not see.

However, the needs of the farm and those who depended on its success forced me back to the reality of needing to provide a good crop each year. Seedtime and harvest have no respect for the melancholic. I was forced back into the necessities of farm life. Nevertheless, more than ever, I anxiously awaited the visits of tradesmen, not for what they sold, but for the news they brought. I listened with rapt attention to tidings of the activities of the Norse in Aenglandi. But two years after I had returned to Borresta, the Danish king, Sven, who they call Split Beard, invaded the country with his huge army.

It was on my annual visit to Aros that, to my amazement, I learned that Sven had become king of Aenglandi, but that he died soon after and his son Knut had taken the throne. The English king, Ethelred, with whom I was so familiar through the portrait on the coins I coveted, had first fled the country and then later returned and ousted Knut. These happenings were both astounding and confusing, for had not Thorkell, the commander I fought for, been defending the English king from invaders? There was news too of huge payments of silver being made by Ethelred to those who defended him.

The news simultaneously distracted me from my work and attracted me to consider the possibility to increase my wealth, reunite with my Saxon son and find his mother. My enthusiasm was fed by rumours spread by travellers, that Knut would try to retake the throne he had lost.

"Onäm, you remember our conversation three winters ago, when I returned with Dag?"

"It was one that filled me with dread."

"How so?"

"I am getting very old, and the farm needs your attention."

"But you managed last time I was away."

"It was not easy, and in any case, I am older now."

"But you have Inger to help, and her son is now grown into a man. He is very clever with his hands and almost as strong as his father was."

There was a silence while Onäm collected his thoughts.

"Have you considered that you have been very fortunate not to be killed in Aenglandi, or even die on the voyages?"

"Yes, but each time I have become more skilled as a warrior."

"But you are older. I think you may have seen forty winters."

"I have made up my mind. It is said that Knut will take an army to Aenglandi next summer to regain the crown."

"And you will join him to fight against Thorkell, to whom you have once sworn allegiance?"

"Yes, I will fight for whoever pays me."

"But you have enough silver for your needs."

"A man can never have enough silver."

"I heard the peddler telling you that Knut is a very cruel commander. He related that when he returned the hostages he had taken, he first cut off their noses, ears, and hands and left them stranded on the beach."

"That may be, but in wartime, cruel things happen."

Onäm had given up persuasion when he emptied his tankard and banged it down heavily on the bench before leaving the room. He had lost the argument and soon after I began to make arrangements for my journey.

There were many times over the next three years when I wished that I had heeded Onäm's words, for it was a period of war and battles such as can never have been seen before in the Kingdom of Aenglandi. And most of the time we were moving from place to place and suffering the privations of a marching force. Just as before, under Thorkell, the invading fleet landed at Sandwich. This time the ships were even more numerous; some men counted one hundred and sixty. Our ship carried one of Knut's officers, Fenir. He and I were of an age and related well in conversation, especially when he learned that I had been in the battles of Maeldun and Ringmere.

"And how would you recommend our commander to act when we land?" he asked me.

"Avoid attacking the city known as Londinium, for it is strong and well defended. Thorkell never took the town."

"So, where would you advise Knut to establish himself first?"

"The heart of the country is in the land of the West Saxons, Wessex. This is only second to Londinium."

I do not know if my advice was heeded, for at first our great army of perhaps six thousand men just roved around the area of Kent, stealing and killing. No Saxon force came to meet us, so we re-embarked and sailed to the river known as Frome in Dorsetshire. There the army landed again, and we exacted plunder as we marched through Somerset and Wiltshire until the West Saxons submitted to Knut.

Serving Knut as a warrior was very different from what we had been used to under other leaders. Very soon after landing this had become apparent. His army was more organised with strict conditions of service, and there was a structure of command such as we had not had before. The officers were chosen by Knut, not by the men. I see now that under Gnir, Toste, and even Thorkell, I was part of an armed, though skilled, rabble who mainly served as long as the commander was successful. Knut appointed commanders and kept very close control that they served him faithfully. Under the commanders there were lower officers who issued orders to us, and discipline was harsh.

When we returned to our ships, we were joined by Earl Edric who had deserted Ethelred and taken with him forty ships. As we lived through the winter on the food and provisions promised to us by the West Saxons, we believed we were now invincible and must take the crown from the Saxon king in the spring. But then the chaos continued, and it became even more bewildering for those of us who were not officers. Our confidence was shaken when Elthelred's son, Edmund, who became known as "Ironside," proved to be a wily adversary. Knut preferred to avoid battle with him and dragged all of us on a long march to Northumberland where he had had the earl, Utred, murdered. And so, the bloody mayhem continued during which Ethelred died and Edmund became king. In the middle of all this, Thorkell changed sides and joined Knut.

After many skirmishes and small battles, the armies of Knut and Edmund finally met at a place called Assunden. We were returning to our ships after the long march south from Northumberland. We had almost reached the river that flows through Londinium, where our ships were moored, when we came upon a great Saxon army blocking our path. I was fortunate, for out of respect for my age I was positioned near Knut in his last reserve. The battle was dreadful. We were on a hill where Knut's standard flew and from where he directed his army. Unlike our commander, King Edmund led his men from the front, and we could see his standard raised in the thick of the fighting. And there was another standard I recognised, that of Ulfyctel, our adversary at Ringmere, the battle where Erik had died. I learned later that Ulfyctel, the leader of the East Anglian army, was killed by Thorkell himself. The fighting was so intense, and the outcome so unclear, that Knut eventually sent the last reserve down the hill to join the fray. We had almost fought ourselves to a standstill with awful losses when Edmund fled the field. The result of this battle of Assunden was as confusing to normal men as many of the things that had happened in the past two years. Two weeks after this slaughter, Edmund and Knut met and declared themselves to be allies and sworn brothers who should share the kingdom. We warriors rejoiced and returned to our ships with the booty we had plundered and made plans to sail back to our homes, but once more things were not as expected. At the end of the eleventh month, Edmund died and Knut declared himself "King of England, Denmark, Norway, and part of Sweden."

The new king proved himself to be as cruel as Onäm had predicted. Many noblemen were murdered and their lands forfeited. We were not allowed to return to the Norse lands, for the army was needed to extend Knut's control of the country. Through my friendship with Fenir, I was given the command of a group of warriors ensuring the subservience of the people of East Anglia. This pleased me as Thorkell had been made Earl of East Anglia and I was once more serving him from our base in Norwic. There was much to be done, for many Saxons, though tired of the continuous warring of the last years, resented Knut's rule. Armed groups harried towns now controlled by the Norse king's officials.

We rode from village to village, seeking out any armed insurgency and warning the inhabitants of the dire consequences if they were to harbour rebels. It was hard to rein in the instincts of my men not to plunder and kill; they were not of a nature that would give the Saxons any faith in the new regime. Though there was discipline they were often wild and cruel. I realised that the Saxons were not people to be cowed and that the effect of our presence would more likely encourage insurrection. Knut recognised this too. To encourage acceptance of his rule he was tolerant of many aspects of Saxon tradition, including religion, for Knut was a follower of the cross, as had been his father and grandfather before him. This was very important to the Saxons, for they were very religious. Where we did find men bearing arms, we killed or captured them and confiscated the produce of the harvest in their villages. We continued with this work all through two winters, after which time the rule of Knut was widely respected by dint of the reprisals taken against those who rejected it, but also because of the tolerance and respect he showed for the Saxon ways.

The last winter I was in Norwic, rumours began to spread among the officers that Knut, now feeling secure as monarch of the country, would disband part of his army and pay us silver to leave. I was longing to return to Ribbagård and waited anxiously for news of this. But I also had another great wish. I had never been able to visit Gippeswic. My orders never permitted me to travel so far south from our base, but now it seemed to me that if the army was disbanded, I might sail home from this port.

It was in the early spring that a large body of armed men guarding a covered cart arrived in Norwic. The rumours had been true. We were to be given the choice to leave the army! The cart contained a shipment of silver to pay off those who agreed to do so. We learned later that Knut had collected seventy-two thousand pounds weight of silver and the town of Londinium had contributed ten thousand pounds more, to fund the disbandonment of his fighting men..

An officer who had arrived with the cart met each of us.

"Who are you and what have you done to deserve a share of the silver?"

"I am Ulf of Borresta, son of Hafnir. Veteran of the Battles of Maeldun, Ringmere, and Assundun."

As I hoped, mention of Assundun got his attention.

"A survivor of our fights with Ulfcytel? You fought him in two battles?"

"Yes, and serving the same commander, Thorkell."

"And now you wish for permission to go home?"

"Yes, I want to sail back to the Norse lands from Gippeswic."

"Gippeswic? Why?"

"Many years ago, I served Olof Tryggvason and Skagul Toste near to Gippeswic. One of my companions was killed there. I wish to visit the place of his death."

"After all this time?"

"Yes."

"This man must have been very special to you."

"A man I will never forget."

"So be it. Take three of your best men to accompany you, as the roads are still not safe. They must leave their silver here, for I want a guarantee that they will return."

"Thank you, Commander."

I left his hut, relieved that I had not been forced to lie to him. Tor was indeed one of my companions, although my greatest enemy. I shuddered when I thought back to how I had killed him in the very place I wished to visit.

As I left, the commander had given me a wooden token that I should take to the cart where my share would be weighed out. When I received it, I was happy. The bag contained much more than the quantity I had earned all those years ago with Toste and Thorkell.

I chose three of the best young warriors in my group. They were very enthusiastic about a task that would relieve the boredom of the winter. We chose good horses but I was soon to find that mine was the worst of them. In view of what had been said about the insecurity of the roads, we wore hauberks of chain mail over our shirts. My silver was problematic. I had a band around each ankle beneath my boots, and the remainder was in two pouches on my belt. A week later I set off with my escorts.

Each evening we stopped at a village and ordered the inhabitants to feed us and provide bedding. While our presence was resented, the people were grateful for not being robbed, or worse. The weather was fine for the most part, and although the trail was wet in places from the winter rains, the horses had no difficulties, although my mare was often spooked and needed careful handling. From time to time, we passed men and women working in the fields, preparing for sowing. They always stopped work at our approach, uncertain whether they should run and seek safety. Although it was three years since I had worked the land myself, I took a great interest in watching the ways of Saxon farmers. I envied the manner in which they could use the plough so early in the year, while at Ribbagård we had to wait for the soil to thaw. They could also keep their cattle and sheep outside all through the year, something we could not do.

And so we proceeded, following a wide trail, which, although it was scored in the middle with deep cart ruts, gave easy riding. Spring flowers bloomed on the edges of the track and our progress was entertained by birdsong. On the fourth day, we knew we would soon reach our destination, for at the last village we had stayed at, villagers had told us so. We were in good heart, but I was getting increasingly worried about how I was going to explain to my companions why I first wished to visit a mill, and indeed I did not want them to accompany me there. I anguished over how to tell them this without raising suspicion and dropped back some distance from them to consider my dilemma in peace without the distraction of their conversation. Deep in thought, I forgot a lesson learnt from Gnir's campaign. Always on our approach, birds would fly up from the thickets; the loud flapping of the larger birds' wings was sometimes alarming, even though we were used to it. I knew that these sounds should be reassuring, not of concern, for it was a sure sign that the birds had not been frightened off by others lying in wait. In my deep concentration about how not to reveal to my companions the real reason for this journey, I did not notice the silence.

As ever, my horse needed a firm rein and, as the attack started, the whoops of the Saxons startled her. She shied away and turned back immediately, breaking into a gallop. There was nothing I could do to support my companions. The attackers had obviously waited until the three warriors had passed them before springing the onslaught and cutting off their retreat.

As I tried to stop the wild beast I was riding, she threw me. I landed heavily to the ground. Fortunately, the mud broke my fall but momentarily I was winded and could hardly move. I struggled to my feet, and in near panic considered my options. The horse had stopped and was now grazing, perhaps two hundred paces away down the track from me. With my heavy hauberk, the silver, and shield, it would take me too long to reach her before the attackers would notice my predicament.

I stood and watched the scene ahead of me. A second group of Saxons was ahead of the three warriors to prevent them escaping. The Norsemen were vastly outnumbered. Still, so far, none of the Saxons had turned to pursue me. Should I try to run to the horse, or could I surrender and tell them that I am seeking Oswald of Ipswich, my son. I had the absurd thought that he may be known to them.

No, the forest must be my refuge.

I threw my shield down and dashed into the woods. I stopped to abandon my hauberk and only then realised that I had strained my left hand. I must have put it down to break my fall from the horse. I gave up dragging the metal mail over my head. The forest was dense. I stumbled over roots and battled against fronds of blackberry bushes that reached out to attach themselves to me. Here and there, between the oaks and beeches, there were almost impenetrable thickets of blackthorn and hawthorn. I chose a thicket and searched for a way in.

Finding a gap, I crawled under the bushes, using my elbows and knees. The hawthorn spikes caught on my hauberk, but they afforded some protection to my back and arms. Not so my hands and knees but I was oblivious to the pain from the scratches.

I gasped for breath as I crawled further in, fighting the sturdy stalks of the bush, each one seeming to catch on the hilt of my buckled sword. At last, hoping that I had hidden myself sufficiently to evade discovery, I carefully rolled over on my back, urging the thicker stems to relent and bend enough to give me space. I tried to sit up, but the undergrowth was too thick. Despite my desperation it was impossible to part the branches to keep a watch. Even the sun hardly penetrated the leaves. I realised that if I could not see out, others could not see in.

There was a strange quiet. Perhaps the Saxons were waiting for them to surrender. Then, suddenly, I could hear the pounding of horses' hooves and the whoops of the Saxon warriors. There could be no escape for my three companions.

I heard the distant thump of sword on shield, the yelps of the hunters, and shrieks as weapons found their mark. The three had no chance, but I knew they would give good account of themselves before they succumbed.

The Saxons would be enjoying teasing the Norsemen as they prepared to slit their throats. Saxon laughter was interspersed by loud curses in my language.

My head hit the ground as I gave up trying to see what was happening and laid back. I was filled with remorse; this was my doing. I should never have allowed my young friends, headstrong as they were, to accompany me.

As I lay there, I considered with regret the foolishness of my venture and what I should do now. The fact that the horse was still on the track, now riderless, would tell the Saxons that I was alive and on foot. But would they look for me? They might be satisfied with their day's work and flee before it was discovered. I considered my options. Going all the way back, alone on foot, was too risky. I must continue, for Gippeswic could not be far away. If I could walk there, I would be safe, for I knew it to be firmly under Knut's control.

I decided to stay where I was for the while; the discomfort was little price to pay if my hiding place saved my life. It was almost dusk when I dared to extricate myself from the bushes, though the sharp thorns were reluctant to permit my escape. The sound of the evening chorus gave me confidence that I was quite alone as I struggled to escape the confine and weight of the hauberk. The injury to my left hand made it difficult to drag the metal vest over my head but, eventually, I could abandon it to nature. I searched around for a tree with a trunk wide enough to give me some shelter and comfort for the night to come, picked some bunches of ferns to lie on, and, as far I could, covered myself with them in the hope that I might get some protection from the cold night air.

After a fitful night's sleep, I cautiously made my way to the track. Despite taking great care with my feet, it was impossible to walk without snapping twigs and creating a noise. But only the birds and animals of the forest would have heard, for the trail was deserted.

I stood at the side of the track, looking in the direction we had come from. There was no sign of the horse. It was difficult to see far in the direction we had been travelling, as there was a bend further on, but I could see the bodies of my companions lying where they had fallen after the Saxons had finished with them. I started walking that way. I had not gone many paces when I heard a noise, a squeaking sound, and voices. A cart, drawn by two donkeys, appeared coming towards me. The driver must have seen me. There was no point in running, so I continued walking.

The cart arrived at the place where my previous companions lay, just before me, and it stopped. I saw that the driver was accompanied by a boy. They were clearly worried to see me and no wonder why. I was fully armed, and my shirt was bloodied by the attention of the thorns.

"Where are you going?" I asked in the Saxon tongue.

"They sent us to get the bodies," said the driver.

"Who did?"

The two of them looked anxiously at each other and, finally, the carter said, "A good Christian man who wants them buried."

"And where does this good Christian man live?"

"In Gippeswic."

I realised that the rumour of the ambush must have reached the town and that perhaps the perpetrators had sent the cart. I looked at the savaged bodies and my feelings of remorse returned. Their hauberks had been removed and their weapons and belts stolen, but they still had their boots on.

"I'll help you," I said.

The two of them got off the cart and surveyed the ghastly scene. The man made a crucifix sign across his chest while the boy tried to avert his eyes from the bodies.

I felt no fear of these two and eased my grip on my sword hilt.

"Let me take their boots off, you can have them," I said.

I knew that there was a good chance that one or more of my companions would have cheated on the requirement to leave their silver at Norwic. Trying to obscure what I was doing, I eased the boots off the first dead warrior. There was no silver in his boots.

"Here, you can keep the boots. They are well made," I said as I handed them to the man.

He took them, examined them, and put them on the cart. The two of them were distracted lifting the heavy stiff body while I removed the left boot from the second warrior. There was a strip of silver wrapped round his ankle. I pulled it off and forced it into one of my belt bags. I made the same discovery on the right ankle.

"Here, take his boots too," I said.

The boots were taken and then the two of them laboured to drag the warrior, the biggest of them, onto the cart. Once more they were distracted as I did my work and added more silver to my bag. I stood up and helped them to lift the third body.

When the loading was finished, I said, "I want to travel to Gippeswic with you."

They looked anxiously at each other, clearly not at ease to have my company, but I left them no choice as I squeezed into a space beside the bodies.

It was not long before we passed a few hovels and signs of habitation. I realised that we must be nearing the town.

"Take me to the mill," I demanded, fingering the knife on my belt.

My request caused my companions to look at each other querulously with resignation, but there was no dissent from them. We passed a similar scene to that which I had seen earlier – men and women working in the fields, here and there cows and other animals in pens, and protesting chickens as we disturbed their rooting in the grass at the side of the track. At a crossroads, the carter turned on to a narrower trail, and as we came over a hillock, I saw the mill on a hill beyond. I suddenly became nervous. What awaited me?

The cart stopped in the yard at the back of the mill house and I jumped off. I waved in thanks to the carter and hesitantly walked around to the front of the building.

CHAPTER 19

The door creaked open as I reached it; clearly the arrival of the cart had been noticed. I don't really know what I was expecting, though I had a foolish hope that I might be greeted by Hana's smile.

I was confronted by a thickset fellow in a jacket completely white with flour, his hair and hands likewise.

"Who are you? What do you want?" said his gruff voice in my own language.

I tried to recover from my surprise as I stuttered, "Why are you here?"

"What do you think, I'm the miller!"

"But you're not Saxon!"

"Where have you been, have you not heard? Knut has banned Saxons from important jobs like milling."

"But what about the people who owned the mill before? Where are they?"

"Why do you want to know, anyway who are you?"

"I am one of Thorkell's officers. I serve him in Norwic."

"Oh, so you'll be looking for Oswald, one of the Saxon rebels who used to live here."

"Yes, where is he?"

"Locked up in the harbour, waiting to be taken to Londinium. They say that Knut wants to have a public execution with as many rebels as he can lay his hands on."

I thought for a moment and then said, "And his mother?"

"Wait, I'll ask one of my Saxon men."

The door closed and I waited outside. The sails of the windmill were creaking as they laboriously turned, powered by the wind they were facing. Down the hill I could see smoke rising from the huts of the village, blown by the same wind. Beyond the huts there were ships in the little harbour and at sea some activity in small boats, probably fishermen.

The door opened.

"They say that she left here even before Swein Forkbeard became king. She entered the nunnery and turned her back on the world."

I tried to hide my disappointment as I said, "Can you sell me a horse?"

"Did Thorkell send you all this way without one?" he said, laughing.

"No, I was robbed."

"Oh, I see. That explains your appearance. Where did it happen?"

"On the road from Norwic."

"Damned rebels. You had good fortune not to have your throat cut."

I did not want to prolong the conversation, so in an assertive tone I said, "Do you have a horse or not?"

"Do you have coin?"

"Yes."

He showed me around to the stable at the back of the mill and we agreed a price for a nag that was so old that he could no longer use her to pull a cart. As I mounted, he said, "Oh yes, Oswald's wife, soon to be widow, lives in the village at her mother's house. At least that's what one of my men told me."

I took leave of the miller and walked the horse slowly towards the village while considering the complexity of the situation I had found myself in. The woman I wanted to meet was a nun, my son was to be executed, and his wife, now my kin, lived nearby.

My priority had to be to save Oswald from execution, so I sought the base of the local Norse commander. It was not difficult to find, as a chieftain's banner was flying in front of a fine building that must have once been the home of a Saxon merchant. My visit to the building was brief. After announcing to a guard that I was an officer from Norwic, I was shown inside and there met Knut's local official. I told him of the robbery, but it was not news to him.

"This area of the country is difficult but soon we'll have cleared the rebels from the region," he told me.

"You have captured some of them?"

"Yes, we're waiting for a few more to be brought in, and then we'll transport them to be executed in Londinium."

"Where are your prisoners?"

"Locked in a building in the harbour, quite secure."

With this knowledge I realised that there would be some time, perhaps days, before Oswald was transported south. When I asked him where the local nunnery was, he roared with laughter and said, "Want a woman do you? Don't try the nunnery, Knut is a Christian and he does not take kindly to shaven heads or nuns being violated. But if you must know, the place is half a day's walk down the track towards Londinium."

"I need to find a ship to take me to the northlands, where can I stay while I wait?"

"The army has taken over the houses by the harbour, you'll find a place to sleep there."

I left him and went to find a place where I could eat and consider what I should do. The sun was at its height, too late to make the journey to the nunnery. I decided to find where Oswald was being held and to ask at the harbour about ships going north. I tied my horse up to a post and sauntered along the quay.

"Are you the master of this ship?" I asked a man sitting on a bench at the stern of a moored vessel.

"I am, and I suppose like many others, you are looking for a way to get home."

"This is true, I can pay silver for my passage."

"And that is what they all say. You're a Svea aren't you?"

My accent easily identified where I came from.

"Yes, does that matter?"

Too late I realised that my tone was aggressive. I was answered assertively.

"Try that ship over there, the crew are your kind. Best you stick with them, I don't want fighting on my boat."

"Do you expect it?"

"There'll be many a man who'll start the journey home with silver in his pouch but will end it in a watery grave with an empty one."

He was right. I had been considering for a long time how to return home with my fortune. The last time I voyaged from Aenglandi I was together with friends. We had protected each other from the thieving instincts and greed of other passengers. This time I was on my own and with much more silver to carry.

I looked at the vessel he had pointed to. It was not a sleek longship like the one in front of me, but a cargo ship, the type they called "knar." I walked alongside and asked one of the crew members working on deck, "Where do you sail to?"

"If the weather is good, to places on the Svea coast and then to trade at Birka."

"When do you leave?"

The men started laughing, and one said, "When the master has found money to buy the cargo."

"What is your cargo?"

"Slaves or thralls you might call them. We'll have a ship full of Saxon troublemakers, all banished from Aenglandi."

At once, I realised the answer to my dilemma was here.

"Where is the master?"

"Captain Anders is spending his money on ale, as usual."

"Or women, or dice!" added another.

"Come and wake him when the cock crows, he'll be in need of silver. You'll get a good price for a passage."

I left the quay and walked along the harbour, looking for the place where the Saxon rebels were held and waiting for transport to Londinium. After asking several people, I was directed to a ramshackle pair of huts. There was a guard outside one of them.

"How many prisoners are there?" I asked.

The guard looked me up and down. It was obvious from the decorated hilt on my sword and the knife strapped across my chest that I was a warrior, but my ragged and bloodied shirt told a different tale.

"Who's asking?" he said brusquely.

"Someone who was robbed by Saxon rebels last night and my companions killed."

Showing me more respect, he answered, "Five, five for Knut's gallows."

I pulled a silver coin from my belt and pressed it into his hand as I whispered, "I want to see the one called Oswald."

He opened his hand and looked at the coin.

"Come with me," he said as he lifted a key on a string tied to his belt. "Over here, in the other hut."

I followed him and watched while he unlocked the door.

"There's just two in here. What's he to you anyway?"

"I fought at the Battle of Ringmere, he was my adversary."

Now with even more respect, he said, "Then you are both lucky to be alive, not that he will be much longer. Don't worry, he's tied up."

He stayed outside while I went in. There was a foul stench in the air that hit me as I stepped inside. It was almost dark, the only light coming through a smoke hole in the roof. "Oswald," I said quietly.

"Who is it who has come to taunt me?" a weak voice replied.

"I am Ulf of Borresta, son of Hafnir. We met at your mother's mill and later on the field of Ringmere."

"So, you survived!"

"As did you, but my best friend did not," I answered.

My eyes were getting used to the darkness and I could now see two figures sitting on straw, their hands tied to the central post that supported the roof.

"You know you are to be executed."

"Yes, by the usurper king. Why are you here?"

"I want to save you, but you are not safe in this country, you must come with me."

"Save me? Why would a Norse want to save me?"

"I have a reason. I am arranging to travel to my land on a ship in the harbour. I can take you with me."

There was a silence. Then a short conversation between the two prisoners. I understood most of it and what Oswald said next confirmed this.

"I can't leave my wife here, or my companion, Aelfric, for he is my wife's brother."

"But if you are executed, your wife will be left here," I blurted clumsily.

"No, no, I will not leave Aelfric to die alone."

I was getting exasperated. My plan was becoming too complicated.

"Very well, I will see what I can do. Both of you be ready to leave next time I come here.

As I was turning to open the door, I paused and said, "What's your wife's name?"

"Wendelin."

"Where can I find her?"

"Our house is near to the water well on the hill, by the road to the mill."

I opened the door and stepped outside into the bright early evening light. The guard walked over to me and pushed the key into the lock.

"I hope you heard what you wanted," he said.

"No, not really. I had hoped that the man would be my thrall, he's a strong fellow. It's too late now. I would have paid a lot to buy him."

"How much?"

"I'd pay twenty aurar for the two of them."

"Would you now?"

"Yes, I would. Think about it, I'll come to see you tomorrow evening. What's your name?"

"Stig, and that's all you need to know." He lifted something on his arm and held it up. "Here, I got this for you. It's a good jacket, I see that you need one. A prisoner who was hung last week doesn't need it now. You can have it for half an aura."

It was indeed true that I needed to cover the bloodied shirt I was wearing. We both laughed. I paid him a coin and went on my way to collect my horse and find a place to sleep.

Next morning at first light, I went to the harbour and stopped by the knar. The sail was stretched over the centre of the ship, the part where cargo would be carried, and it was apparent from the lumps in the woollen cloth that there were people underneath, still sleeping.

"Captain Anders, I want to speak with you!" I shouted.

There was no response, so I tried again. This time I saw one of the lumps move, and when it reached the edge of the sail a head appeared.

"You accursed swine, why do you wake me so early!"

"I need to talk to you about an urgent matter."

"Urgent! What's so urgent that a man can't sleep off his ale?"

By this time the dishevelled man was standing in front of me. He was not an impressive figure. His long hair was tangled and matted. He brushed it from his face and glowered at me with eyes almost the colour of cherries, the same hue as his cheeks.

I held up a hand in an attempt to still any further outburst, but he had not finished.

"I am the captain of this fine vessel and I expect to be respected, not dragged out of my bed before the cock crows."

"And I am an officer in the army of King Knut who is used to settling scores with the edge of my sword or the tip of my knife. Now be silent and step ashore to speak with me in private."

The man coughed loudly to clear his throat and then spat on the deck of his ship before clambering over the gunnel.

When we were out of earshot of any listeners still under the sail, I said, "I understand that you trade with slaves. Have you bought any to take north?"

"What business is that of yours?"

"Simply that I want to charter your ship. I'd pay a good price in silver."

"The whole ship?"

"Yes."

"Where do you want to go?"

"Aros. Do you know it?"

"Oh yes, I've travelled through it many times with cargoes of iron. We stop there before making for Tälje and then the open sea."

"I want to leave tonight, when it is dark."

"Impossible. The waterway out of here to the sea is narrow and difficult to navigate even in daytime. At night it would be impossible. In any case, the tide must be right for us to cross the shallows."

I quickly considered how to get around these difficulties.

"When will the sea be deep enough?"

The captain walked to the edge of the wooden quay and looked at the water.

"The tide's ebbing now. Tomorrow it will be a bit later, so at first light we should be able to sail."

"Then before sunrise. I will need to hide my friends under the sail through the night."

"Who are they?"

"You need not know. Well, what's your price? There'll be four or five of us."

The man scratched his scruffy beard and looked over my shoulder, staring at the morning sky while he thought.

"Sixty auror."

"Too much, I'll talk to the captain of the ship over there."

As I started to walk away, he grabbed my arm and said, "Wait, I have reconsidered the matter. I could go on from Aros up to the great river and then north to the iron makers to get a return cargo. Fifty auror."

"Forty."

"For a fine officer of King Knut's army, forty-five."

"Agreed. Twenty when we leave and twenty-five when we arrive."

"So be it."

"Have the ship ready to leave at first light and it may help your navigation if you leave the ale to others tonight."

For the first time, he grinned.

I was well pleased with our agreement. The silver I had taken from the dead warriors would cover the cost of the voyage and my fortune would be left untouched. That was my first task of the day accomplished, and now I could embark on the one I had been longing for most.

I collected my horse and mounted. Reluctantly, she broke into a trot, and we weaved our way through the village and up the hill to find the road to Londinium. Part way up, I noticed the long wooden beam over the well Oswald had told me about. The ends were rising and falling as the queuing women took their turn to fill their buckets.

It was not difficult to identify the nunnery. It stood a little way off the roadside, surrounded by a wooden fence. The gate was open, so I walked my horse to the door of the stone-built house, dismounted, and tied her to a ring on the wall. The large front door was closed so I beat the hilt of my knife on it several times. Eventually, a small flap in the door was slid open and a female voice demanded to know my business.

"I am Ulf of Borresta, son of Hafnir, and servant of King Knut. I wish to speak with Sister Hana."

There was a long pause before the voice spoke again, "Why do you wish to see the sister?"

"I have news of her son."

"I must speak with the Abbatissa," said the voice as the small flap was slid closed.

My heart was beating fast, even faster than I remember it did as we waited for the charge at Assundun. I stood rubbing the scar on my neck, nervously considering what I should do if I was not permitted to see Hana.

After a long wait, the flap slid open and the voice said, "The Abbatissa will see you."

There was the sound of a metal bolt being drawn, and soon after, the door opened to reveal a nun. She beckoned me to follow her and led the way down a corridor and through a door to a cloister. The place seemed completely deserted, but I realised that all of the nuns had probably been sent to their cells to avoid contact with a male outsider. A door in front of me was opened by an elderly nun who bade me enter the room. She was much shorter than me and I found myself peering down at her. She made no attempt to make eye contact, keeping her face mostly hidden by her white cap.

"I understand that you wish to see Sister Hana. Why?"

"I have news of her son, Oswald. I met him last night."

"Sister Hana has been here for many years. She is very unworldly, and I cannot think that she would want to hear news of a son she has long forgotten."

"A mother never forgets children she has begat."

"Is your news good?"

"Yes, it will be."

"Are you a follower of Christ?"

I was not prepared for this question, though I should have been.

"Not yet, but I may become so."

"Yet, you show the charity, which is a feature of our faith, in wishing to impart your news to a Christian mother."

I made no comment but stood in silence, filled with hope.

"You may wait in the cloister."

I turned and left the room, retracing my steps to the open-air place. There I waited. There was no sound, but I could feel that there were many pairs of eyes watching me from the cells around the circular space.

Then I heard the clang of a metal latch opening. I turned to the cells behind me from whence the sound had come. The door of one of them opened and a figure appeared, accompanied by the Abbatissa. Hana walked towards me, and the senior nun left her to complete the distance alone.

I knew that I could not, nor should not, throw my arms around her but every instinct in my body told me to do so. I resisted. She stood in front of me, head bowed and silent.

I kept my voice as quiet as I could, trying to keep my words private.

"It has been a long time, for almost thirty years I have longed to see you."

An even quieter voice replied, "You have news of our son?"

I was sorely disappointed that her words were not as tender as mine.

"Yes, he has been fighting against the new king of England."

"This does not interest me, tell me of his welfare."

215

It was as if I was winded in battle, for I could hardly speak. I longed for her to raise her head so that I could see her face. Her long black hair had been cropped but I could see from the strands protruding from her cap that the colour had not changed.

As tenderly as I could, I replied, "He is well, but he is to be executed by this king."

"It is not the will of God that he should die young."

"He will not, for I will save him and take him from these shores."

"I will pray for you."

"Will you not come too?"

"I cannot, for I am married to God. It is the way of my faith."

"But you can follow your faith even if you come with me."

"It is too late. I waited for you. Now is too late, for I have taken vows."

There was the sound of another voice, that of the Abbatissa.

"It is time for you to leave us, Ulf of Borresta," she commanded as she walked towards us.

And then it happened; Hana raised her head and looked straight at me. Her face showed her age; there were wrinkles and her dark skin had some blemishes. But her eyes told me everything about her true feeling. They were the same dark mesmerising eyes that I had once loved and still did, but they were filled with tears, tears that then ran down her cheeks.

She was ushered away, back in the direction of her cell. I watched as she opened the door. She turned as she entered, and I fancied, yes I know, that I saw a smile.

After leaving the nunnery, my feeling of deep despondency was partially lifted by the thought of meeting my son's wife, Wendelin. I retraced the journey back to where I had seen the well. There was still a queue, though it was shorter, and I stopped alongside it. The women looked up at me with fear in their eyes, fear that I was Norseman who might violate them, or just nervousness about what I, a foreigner whose master has taken over the crown, represented, I know not. Perhaps it was both.

"Where can I find Wendelin?" I asked the nearest woman.

She looked around at the others. I realised that she feared that Wendelin might be associated with her husband's felony and that I threatened her freedom. She did not want to be the one in the queue who betrayed Oswald's wife.

There were no answers to my question. I needed to use a better approach.

"I have been to see Oswald and have good news about him for Wendelin."

This time, there was chattering in the queue, and eventually an old woman was urged by the others to speak to me.

"She lives with her mother now, over there."

The woman slowly and hesitantly raised her hand, directing my attention to a turf-covered hut not far away. I raised my hand, indicating thanks to the speaker, and turned my horse in that direction. There was smoke coming out through the smoke hole at the top of the hut. There must be someone in the house. I got off my horse and led him towards the hut.

I knocked on the door and called out, "I have news of Oswald, your husband."

The door opened a little way, and someone peered out but when I moved forward the door slammed in my face. I was conscious of the rapt attention of the queue of women some way behind me. I had to speak quietly, as my message for Wendelin was private.

I tried again, this time saying, "I have important news of Oswald that may save his life!"

The door opened and a young woman came out. Showing no fear of me, she said, "Is it not enough that you have taken my husband, that now you pursue me?"

With careful words I was soon able to calm Wendelin and explain my plan.

CHAPTER 20

Some time before dusk, I returned to the harbour. A busy scene greeted me. It was clear that I was not the only warrior who had recently left the king's service. Crowds of fully armed men carrying their shields on their backs over their belongings were clamouring to make bids to the captains of the vessels in the harbour for a passage back to the northlands. Through the shouting, cursing, and general hubbub I heard the absurd prices some ships' masters were demanding for a thwart on the ships, some of which appeared hardly seaworthy. I began to worry that Captain Anders might become greedy and be tempted either to break our agreement altogether or demand more payment from me. I noted that the knar seemed less attractive to the intending travellers as it was obviously a slower ship. There were few warriors calling out to the crew of the cargo vessel to ask the price of a passage.

I had previously seen that there were three crew on the knar. I would have expected to have seen them busying around preparing for the voyage, but instead they were playing dice on board. There was no sign of Anders. They did not recognize me as I stood by the side of the would-be travellers vying for a place on the ship.

I called out, "Are you not filling the water barrels for your voyage?"

Before being pushed aside by the growing crowd, I heard the curious reply, "We don't need much water for our voyage," amid laughter from the others. The comment concerned me, but my attention was drawn instead to ensure that the same guard was on duty by the buildings where the prisoners were held. As I walked down the quay towards the two wooden buildings, I saw, to my horror, that there were now two guards. One was Stig, with whom I had previously spoken, but the other I had not seen before.

As I approached, Stig smiled and said to the other, quite loudly, "This is the warrior I told you about, a veteran of Ringmere and Assunden."

The other asked, "Did you see Knut in the battle?"

"Yes, from a distance, but he organised his army from behind the battle. I saw King Edmund too, close up. He fought like a mad dog."

The guard I had not met before then said coyly, "You had an interest in two of our prisoners."

"Yes, I said I would pay twenty auror of silver for them."

"Well, we might be able to help, but it is risky for us."

I became alarmed. I was prepared to kill the guard if things went wrong, but it would be much more difficult now there were two of them.

"So, we want twenty auror each."

His demand enraged me, but I tried to stay calm. At least they were prepared to do business.

"Your price is very high, the men will be good thralls, but I am not sure that I want to pay so much."

I waited for them to lower their price, but they stayed silent. After some time, I said, "It's agreed. I will come back when darkness falls. I need a lantern to take inside to cut the ropes."

The men smiled at each other, and we grasped hands. I was not smiling. Leaving them, I returned to the village to find food and to sell my horse.

As soon as dusk had fallen, I returned to the harbour, pushing my way through the crowds of drunken warriors, some junketing, some brawling. My companion had a dark cloak with a cowl covering any hair that might be seen. When we arrived on the quay, I saw from a distance that the two guards were standing by the wall of one of the buildings, a lit lantern hanging there. I could see that they had tankards in their hands.

"Wait here," I said to my companion as we passed the knar.

When approached, they greeted me with slurred speech. It seemed that they had already started celebrating the silver they were to receive.

"Here's a lantern," said Stig as he lifted it from the hook on the wall. By the light of it, the other tried with difficulty to find the keyhole in the door. When he at last opened it, Stig shouted, "Wait, wait! Our silver first."

I had counted out coins and had them ready in a pouch, but I was taking no chances.

"Here, you have half of the amount. The rest I'll give to you when you have released the men."

Stig grabbed the coins and held the lantern up to look at them.

"All right, we'll be waiting."

I took the lantern and entered the building. The two prisoners were momentarily blinded by the light but moved forward so that I could reach the ropes holding them. When they were free, I said, "Follow me outside. The two guards will try to rob me; you take my knife, Aelfric, and, Oswald, use my sword. Use the weapons if they try to cheat me while I pay them."

I led the way out and, sure enough, the two men were waiting, knives in hand.

"You don't think we would risk our necks for forty auror of silver, do you?" said Stig.

"Hand over the pouches on your belt," said the other.

Neither of them had noticed the two supposedly unarmed Saxons moving one behind each of them.

I heard the sound of the sword parting the air as it descended on Stig's shoulder. His scream was quickly followed by the moan from his companion as Aelfric plunged my knife into his back. Both men collapsed to the ground in front of me. I held up the lantern and said to Aelfric, "Take their knives and cut the pouch from the belt of the man you stabbed."

I took my knife back and put the recovered silver into my bag.

"Help me drag them into the hut," I said.

We left both bodies inside, and I locked the door before throwing the key into the river.

Carrying the lantern, I walked back along the harbour and there, waiting in front of the knar, was the hooded figure. Hearing our approach and seeing the light from the lantern, she threw back the hood, revealing the braids hanging on both sides of her head. Both men embraced Wendelin in turn.

"Hurry now, we must embark on the ship and hide under the sail. We leave at first light."

Our arrival had been heard by the crew, and in the lantern light I could see them pulling back the sail from the cargo place.

"You must stay there until we are out of the harbour."

"Where are we going?" asked Oswald.

"As I told you, you are going to my country in the northlands. You will be safe there until you can return to Aenglandi."

My explanation seemed to suffice, for they asked no more questions and hid as told. For my part, there was no need to hide, as my business was quite legal.

"Which thwart shall I take, Anders?" I asked.

"Come and sit in the stern near to me."

I made myself comfortable and prepared to get some sleep before we left in the morning.

"Are you going to tell me who my passengers are?" he asked in a very direct fashion.

"No, that is my business."

"You said you would pay me twenty auror before we leave."

"I will, in the morning."

I was conscious of the fact that if he got silver now, he would go off to celebrate. In his cups, he might well tell others of strangers hidden on his ship.

I was woken long before dawn by a scratching sound. I realised that the noise was coming from the bag I normally carried on my back, that was beside me. It was totally dark; I could see nothing. Something or someone was rummaging in my bag. I slowly stretched out my arm and then grabbed the bag. As I pulled it towards me, there was at first some resistance and then a sound as someone let go and clumsily moved away from my sleeping place. I said nothing, but the realisation dawned on me that this voyage could be an unpleasant one.

At first light the crew was busy preparing for sea.

"Now we need the sail, so your passengers will have to move," said Anders to me.

I roused the sleepers and helped to mount the heavy sail, made of wool with a grease coating, on to the yard arm, which supported it when hoisted. For the first time, the captain saw the three Saxons. He immediately realised that they were not northerners.

"I'll not ask the reason for you to have these three with you, but they will have to help with the management of the ship, the woman too."

"That's understood, Captain," I replied.

Within a short time, we were on our way down the river.

"If you have stolen these three thralls, then soon the owner won't be able to chase us, the tide is ebbing fast and no ship can pass the shallows until the next tide."

I realised that Anders was trying to ascertain from my reply what the status of the three Saxons was, so I did not reply.

By the time the sun had risen, we were out of the river and into the North Sea. As was usual going north, the wind was blowing us in the direction we needed to travel, though it was so strong that the sail was reefed smaller than its normal size by tying part of the cloth to the boom. From my previous voyages I knew that this was a normal thing to do to lessen the chance of a vessel capsizing. All was well, though I was uneasy about the fact that all the crew were armed. The three of them were reasonably friendly to me, but brusque and unhelpful to the Saxons. It was obvious from my passengers' clumsy efforts to assist that they had never been on a ship before.

My unease was compounded when I went forward to get a drink of water. There were three water barrels, but only one of them was full. I realised too that there were few provision barrels. There could hardly be enough food for eight people on a long voyage.

Later, I moved down the ship to mention this to the captain, who was steering the vessel.

"Captain, why do we have so little water and food on board?" I asked bluntly.

"We have enough for our voyage," he growled at me. "If needs be, we can go ashore in some harbour to get more."

"I understand," I said, not wishing to start an argument.

"Tell your passengers to stay in the hold. This ship is designed to have weight there, normally cargo, to keep it balanced. The wind is getting stronger."

I did not pursue the matter further but my suspicions were heightened. I later took Oswald aside and had a talk with him. As I did so, I noticed the captain watching me.

As usual on a voyage to the northlands, the ship was sailing with the coast just in sight on the left side. Occasionally we passed other vessels going in the opposite direction but soon we were alone without a sail in sight. We were making good progress out of shelter of the land with the increasing wind now on the side of the ship.

Soon, the captain shouted an order to the crew to shorten the sail more. They slackened the rope that held the yard arm up and rolled up more sail before raising the yard arm again, this time to halfway up the mast. Nevertheless, the ship was leaning considerably with the pressure of the wind on the shortened sail. The captain was gripping the steering oar with all his strength.

I noticed the crew casting anxious glances at the captain. Then I saw him shake his head. What could that mean? As the ship ploughed through the waves rocking and rolling violently, I kept turning to glance at the crew to see if I could detect what his message might mean.

A little later, one of the crew, a very rough looking fellow with a scar on his left cheek, made his way back to the stern and exchanged some words with Anders. Then he made his way forward as far as the hold and stood behind Wendelin. Things happened very quickly.

I was sitting on my thwart facing the stern. I saw the captain nod to the crew. Turning round to see what was happening behind me, I saw the biggest of the crew members, with difficulty on the pitching ship, making his way towards me, a long knife in his hand.

There was a scream; the rough fellow had grabbed Wendelin by her plaits and was dragging her towards the bow with one hand and holding a knife against her throat with the other. The two Saxons had drawn their knives, the ones we had taken from the guards, but could do nothing for fear of Wendelin being murdered.

At my age, I was in no way able to safely face combat with the strong, young crew member coming towards me. There was no doubting that I was his target. His progress was slowed by having to use one hand on the gunnel to steady himself as he worked his way along the ship on the opposite side from which the wind was blowing. It was the side of the leaning vessel closest to the sea.

I got up and as quickly as I could, with the weight of silver in my boots, precariously made my way to the stern. If the man with the knife caught up to me there was no escape. At the steering oar the captain was helpless; he had to keep control of the ship and could only watch as I came towards him. I slashed at his throat with my knife, and as he fell I grabbed the oar and pushed it away from me with all my might. The heavy ship responded by turning closer to the wind and heeling dangerously. The man pursuing me dropped his knife and in panic tried to grab the gunnels to save himself from the sea, which was now gushing into the ship. He was too late. I watched as we passed him attempting to grab a hold on the hull.

I pulled the oar towards me to take the ship off the wind and avoid a total capsize. My view of the bow was obscured by the sail but as the ship recovered and became upright, I saw Oswald and Aelfric leap from the shallow hold and rush forward. A second crew member, this one oozing blood, had floated past the stern. I later learned that the scar-faced crew member, previously with hands occupied by holding a knife and Wendelin, dropped both to steady himself when the ship heeled over. The two Saxons had seen their chance and quickly dispatched him. The surviving crew member was now sitting dejectedly on a thwart, awaiting his fate.

We spared the man's life as he had knowledge of how to sail the ship. His name was Leif and he proved to be very valuable to us. He told us that it had been the captain's plan to murder us all for my silver and then return to Gippeswic to offer his services to others who wished to journey home.

We had very little food for the three days at sea, and our voyage to the Geat fortress was a hungry one. Once there, we were able to re-provision and embark on the voyage around the coast, first to the south and then, after rounding the southern headland, the long passage north to Aros.

I returned home a very wealthy man, but realised that I was now too old to return to Aenglandi to seek more silver, and gave up the hope too that I might bring Hana to Borresta. I comforted myself by taking one of my slave girls to wife. In quick succession she bore two sons whom we called Karlbjörn and Karsi. They are fine boys, but I still sorely miss Dag and Halvdan.

Apart from my expanding farm I needed another way to increase my wealth. As well as a considerable amount of silver,

I now owned a cargo ship. The vessel allowed me to follow a notion I had had for a long time. For many years now the ship has been used, under the command of Captain Leif, to transport iron from the land of the dales, in the north, to Aros, where it is sold to eager merchants from the south.

CHAPTER 21

"Master, 'tis finished!"

I lifted my head to look at the man addressing me, and, emerging from my sleep, to grasp reality.

"Help me up, I must look closer," I said to the rune maker.

He helped me to my feet and supported me as I shuffled over to the great stone. I peered at the patterns and the symbols for a long time, running my fingers over the contours. I could not betray the fact that my old eyes could no longer make out intricate carvings. My eyes, eyes that once could see a wren in a thicket, no longer served me with details. So, it was by touch that I could be sure that the master rune maker had done his work well. And he had.

"You have skills almost as good as mine, Öpir."

He laughed and then said, "Then you are satisfied with my work, Master?"

"Yes, you can begin the painting. Help me back to my chair. I will watch you."

Sitting, I looked on as he ground the red ochre to make the first colour. It was slow work, and my mind began to stray.

I have lived through many winters and summers. Many more than anyone I know. No one has had my good fortune, though some deserved to live longer. Onäm suffered the disgrace for a warrior of dying in his bed, though I am sure that his past exploits would have found favour with the Valkyries, and he would have been permitted entrance to Valhalla.

Halvar died even before he became a man, and even today I ask why was he taken from me. Have I been given the years he should have had? And Dag too, he died many years before his time. His blindness made him foul tempered and increasingly bereft of reason. For a time, when I gave him a slave girl to warm his bed, he calmed, but his fits eventually forced us to keep his hands tied and sometimes even his feet. Though he sired two children with the thrall, a girl and a boy, he died unrequited. Am I unrequited too? No, surely not, for it is only those who have never loved who die in that state. And apart from my affection for my family and good friends of whom I have told, I have two loves, though I could call them desires or even obsessions. Which is strongest: my desire for wealth or that for the woman? While I have nearly satisfied the former, my desire for Hana lives on in strong measure. It is no longer a desire driven by passion, for when the years wear away the heart rending, punishing feeling which people call passion, if affection remains, it must be love.

Since returning from my service for Knut all those years ago, my growing throng of kinfolk has taken over the work of running my estate of Ribbagård and allowed me much time to sit by the fire and ruminate. Too much time. Some years ago, recalling what Onäm had once suggested about a rune memorial to my achievements, I brought the rune master, Öpir of Aros, to stay at my estate for a long summer and to teach me his skills. Over the following years I created several rune stones, including one in memory of Onäm. Finally, as I realised that my stiff hands would soon prevent me from forming the tangle of snakes and imaginary beasts, I carefully crafted one last memorial. The runes would tell those who stopped to look at it, "Erik, son of Mundr, died a hero's death in Aenglandi."

Now, my memorial is being carved by Öpir. It will be the finest he has ever made. I will leave it to Karlbjörn and Karsi to decide where they should place it, but I hope that it is not far from that of Erik's.

Now the paint is being mixed for the rune stone that, for many hundreds of years will tell those who come after me of my achievements and how I, Ulf of Borresta, lived and fought to satisfy the want of silver.

The Borresta Rune Stone

The runes tell, "Ulf of Borresta gained
a tribute in England three times. Once under **Toste,**
once under **Thorkell** ... and once under **Knut.**"

ACKNOWLEDGEMENTS

I have known of this runestone for a long time, but the story it relates has always worried me. I was concerned about its veracity. How could anyone survive three return journeys over inhospitable terrain and the North Sea, in those brutal and turbulent days? Further, it really vexed me to understand how the massive Danegelds were shared out between warriors and brought back safely to their villages. I got useful advice from various sources to help convince me. Not least from the Stockholm Historical Museum. Thanks are due to the staff who gave me of their time. As for the background material and information about the Asa religion beliefs, I have been fortunate enough to be able to derive ideas from visiting many Scandinavian museums and the sites mentioned in the book. Indeed, it was a visit to Borresta and the feel of the actual rune stone, which eventually persuaded me to tell how Ulf's life might have played out.

Thanks are due to the Sollerön Viking Group for welcoming me as a member. Being able to see and handle artefacts from the Viking grave site on the Island, was inspirational.

My dear wife of over fifty years, Barbro, as ever, has been my companion through the research journeys on land and sea, whatever the weather. She has tolerated and at times, sensibly moderated my enthusiasms. I am so grateful to her for not only reading and commenting on various versions and the final manuscript of this novel, but also advising on the plot.

ABOUT THE AUTHOR

Michael E Wills was born on the Isle of Wight, UK, and educated at Carisbrooke Grammar and St Peter's College, Birmingham. After a long career in education, as a teacher, a teacher trainer and textbook writer, in retirement he took up writing historical novels. His first book, *Finn's Fate*, was followed by a sequel novel, *Three Kings – One Throne*. In 2015, he started on a quartet of Viking stories for young readers called, Children of the Chieftain. The first book, *Betrayed*, was described by the Historical Novel Society reviewer as "An absolutely excellent novel which I could not put down" and long-listed for the Historical Novel Society 2016 Indie Prize. The second book in the quartet, *Banished*, was published in December 2015 followed in 2017 by the third book, *Bounty*. *Bound For Home* completed the series in 2019. His book for younger children, Sven and the Purse of Silver, won bronze medal in the Wishing Shelf Book Awards. His most recent books are from periods in history with an enormous time span between them. *Izar, The Amesbury Archer*, (runner-up for indie historical fiction book of the year 2021) is based in the Neolithic period. a Viking story, *For the Want of Silver*, is based on the message carved on an actual runestone and an award winning series of children's books called *Clifftop Farm In Wartime*, is about WW2.

Though a lot of his spare time is spent with grandchildren, he also has a wide range of interests including researching for future books, writing, playing the guitar, carpentry and electronics.

You can find out more about Michael E Wills and the books he has written by visiting his website: www.michaelwills.eu

OTHER BOOKS
BY MICHAEL E WILLS

(available at www.michaelwills.eu)

Izar, **The Amesbury Archer** This is the story of a man who lived 4,500 years ago. His skeleton is in Salisbury Museum. He was born in the region of the Swiss Alps and died nearly a thousand miles away in the south of England near to Stonehenge, when it was being built. The mystery is how this could have happened, for the man's skeleton shows that he was physically disabled.

He lived at the end of an era, when human curiosity was pushing the boundaries into a new age. It was an exciting time when dependence on stone gave way to a new, more versatile material – metal.

The numerous items buried with the man give tantalising clues as to his ability as an archer, but also to his role as a pioneer metal worker.

> *"Izar's life has been moulded around what little is known about him, and the result is a novel full of intense detail with a gripping narrative."*
> *The Coffee Pot Book Club"*

Finn's Fate tells the story of three brothers in tenth century Scandinavia. Their home is north of the Arctic Circle in an isolated region populated by the Sami, the Laplanders. The living is harsh and the climate unforgiving. After a disastrous fire at their homestead, they decide to ignore their family's wishes and abandon their home. The young men embark on a journey to find a better life. They undertake a lengthy odyssey through unfriendly territory and dangerous seas. Through storms and battles they support each other and become increasingly wealthy as they raid the unprotected villages and ports on the British coast. Their success leads them to a dangerous level of confidence and they embark on one raid too many. The book mirrors actual historical events and offers a solution to a real mystery in the Dorset countryside.

"It's an extremely gripping book that entices the reader to keep going onto the next chapter despite the clock now reading 2am." – The Historical Novel Society

Three Kings – One Throne The eleventh century was the most turbulent time in English history with six kings in sixty years. "Three Kings, One Throne" charts the lives of characters real and imaginary who get caught up in the maelstrom of treachery, carnage, greed, lust and loyalty. In part the novel describes the true story of how the most successful and experienced soldier of the eleventh century, once a member of the elite bodyguard of the Turkish Emperor, launched the biggest ever invasion of England with sixteen thousand men in three hundred ships. An invasion which dwarfed that of Duke William of Normandy in October 1066.

The crown of England was the most contested in Europe, this is the story of three men; two kings and one duke, soon to be a king, and the men and women who fought and died for their causes.

"Michael Wills has done an admirable job in bringing together all the intricate historical details and has woven a credible tale of adventure and political skulduggery." – Jaffa Reads Too

The Wessex Turncoat Aaron Mew is a seventeen year-old apprentice blacksmith living in a small English village, in the late eighteenth century. His life is simple yet secure, until the day when he volunteers to take the place of his father on an errand for the squire. The country boy is wrenched from the environment in which he grew up and thrust into a world of ruffians, drunks, criminals and disgraced professionals – part of the army of George III. An army desperately short of men, but with the huge ambition to quell the rebellion in America and to retain the country under British rule.

After relentless training, Aaron's regiment, the 62nd Regiment of Foot, is posted to Canada. There, fighting side by side with First Nation braves and German allies, the boy soldier becomes a hardened warrior.

The *Wessex Turncoat* tells the story of an ambitious military campaign and the fate of a regiment which was sacrificed mainly because of the vanity and intransigence of an English general.

"I can't stress enough the how I loved the expertise and the countless research hours put into each and every page, as well as the quality of the

dialogue of ordinary soldiers." Alaric Longward, The Review, USA

One Decent Thing Aberystwyth in 1971, Scottie, a self-centered, decadent university administrator with a weakness for cigarettes, drink and women, finds that he is unwelcome when he visits his university student daughter, Tina. His effort to drown his sorrows leads him into a world of terrorism and danger where he becomes a fugitive from the police and from the IRA. In desperation and with the help of some university students, he decides to break with his egocentric habits and do one decent thing. But he has made powerful enemies and will have to face retribution.

"A very enjoyable and exciting book. As the book goes on, it gets increasingly more tense and I found myself reading quickly to see what happens next! The action is well-paced and left me on the edge of my seat"

Ingram Content Group UK Ltd.
Milton Keynes UK
UKHW040637220523
422126UK00001B/9

9 781739 858858